"Rodowsky's style is clear and unpretentious. The difficulty and ambivalence in close relationships are wonderfully dramatized in alternating narratives."
—STARRED / *Booklist*

"A cast of beautifully realized complex characters . . . a first-rate title." —*School Library Journal*

"Rodowsky's tour de force arouses one's passionate feelings in the most memorable of all her award winners." —*Publishers Weekly*

"A fine and moving story." —*The Horn Book*

An ALA Best Book for Young Adults

A School Library Journal
Best Book for Young Adults

Julie's Daughter

BOOKS BY COLBY RODOWSKY

Julie's Daughter

Colby Rodowsky

aerial fiction
Farrar, Straus and Giroux

Copyright © 1985 by Colby Rodowsky
All rights reserved
Library of Congress catalog card number: 85-47589
Published in Canada by HarperCollinsCanadaLtd
Printed in the United States of America
First edition, 1985
Aerial edition, 1992

To my daughters
ALICE, EMILY, KATE,
LAURA *and* SARAH
with love

Julie's
Daughter

Slug

THE STORM came up without any warning and filled the kitchen with chunky gray shadows that lunged out of the corners, making the room suddenly more crowded than when there had been just the two of us—Julie and me. Wind whipped through the open windows and sent the Sunday paper flying and slammed one door after another in the upstairs hall. We pushed back our chairs and ran, closing windows and wiping at puddles with anything we could find.

We stood at the living-room window and watched the water race in torrents down the hill and listened to the wind as it whistled through the walls. I had never been afraid of storms—and wasn't now—but this was a storm and a half, and for a minute I wanted to move closer to Julie as we stood there side by side.

"Gussie loved storms," I said without thinking. And because it felt weird to be talking about Gussie, who had been my grandmother and Julie's mother, I pulled away so that we were standing apart from each other, and even when a tree out front came crashing down we stayed where we were.

The tree fell and the storm ended, in one great burst, like the grand finale of the fireworks display back home. Then the sun came out. It blazed across the sky and made everything up and down the street thick and steamy, so that when we stepped out onto the porch the heat settled over us, and from down at the stream-bed came the roaring of water.

Julie

"WELL, THIS is as good a way as any to meet the neighbors," I said, hating the flipness in my voice and unable to do anything about it. "Just call it 'drum roll with flourishes.'" I looked at Slug, the stranger who had been in my house only since this morning and whose odd-lot assortment of bags and parcels was still heaped just inside the doorway to my spare room. I waited for her to say something, and when she didn't I led the way down off the porch and onto the sidewalk.

"Ernestus Stokes," I said as we watched a woman walk down the street and up over the fallen tree, stepping as if to an unspoken cadence count.

"Mattie-Miller—said all in one breath—and Mr. Bigelow. He grows enormous zinnias and dahlias and even sunflowers. And the Nortons from across the street—mother and father and son, David.

"Get a good look at David while you can, because generally all anybody can see are his feet sticking out from under that orange Pinto over there."

For a few minutes they wandered around, poking at

the tree and ruffling the branches, calling back and forth about how lucky we were that it hadn't fallen *on* anything and how we'd have to call the city to come take it away. Just as they were ready to head back to their own houses, I took a deep breath and said, "This is my daughter, Slug, just come to stay—Slug October, from Virginia." I figured they ought to know right off that her last name wasn't the same as mine.

Ernestus Stokes said she was glad, for my sake, that Slug had come, and that having young people around really did something for a house.

Marian and Tom Norton shook hands and talked about petunias and baseball and other things that people talk about when they have nothing to say.

"Why, Julie Wilgus, what a surprise," Mattie-Miller said, clapping her hands and then stopping short as if she realized that she had said what they were all thinking but were too polite to actually *say*. "Oh my, yes indeed. It *is* nice," she finally went on, her voice settling lightly like fuzz from a dandelion.

Meanwhile, David was standing there eyeing Slug, taking in her high cheekbones, her long dark hair; the way she was awkward and graceful both at the same time.

Ernestus Stokes called everyone to come and take a look at the size of the tree roots, and they moved off, so that it was only Slug and I who saw Harper, leaning on a walking stick, come around from the back of her house on the other side of the street. Her little red dog jumped in front of her as she stepped onto the sidewalk.

"That's Harper Tegges, the artist," I said. "Famous, from what I hear. Someday during the summer we'll go to the museum to see her paintings, if you'd like."

For a minute it was as if the three of us were frozen there: Harper Tegges, Slug, and me. Then Harper fell, lurching forward and down.

Slug yelled and started to run, with me just beside her. I heard the rest of them following along behind.

Harper

It's FUNNY the way it happened. It was almost as if I were standing back watching myself set out with Ginger and my walking stick, and that funny feeling in my foot I'd noticed from time to time. Well, I saw not only myself but the neighbors, too. Bit by bit. Julie Wilgus and Slug October—that newly arrived daughter of hers the mailman told me was coming. He delivers news faster than he delivers mail. Ernestus Stokes holding forth about the tree. David, out from under that car for once and ogling the girl. His mother, looking just like one of those droopy-faced petunias she's forever planting. I hate petunias. Flowers shouldn't droop—any more than people should. I've never painted a droopy flower yet. Even Bigelow's zinnias have pluck.

All the while I could see them, and see me. It was as if I knew I was going to fall, and couldn't do anything to stop it. Like running pell-mell down a hill.

And I did. Fall. Flat down. Face to face with the sidewalk, all gritty and rough-edged under me. For a minute there, I was stunned. Immobile. Staring down at the stupidest ant you've ever seen, worrying about whether this ant was going to get where he wanted to go before someone stepped on him.

Footsteps. It was as if Butternut Street rumbled beneath me. I looked up and there was the girl Slug galloping toward me like a gazelle, the others in hot pursuit.

"She fell. Somebody do something."

"Miss Tegges, are you all right?"

"Lie still now. Everyone get back and give her air."

"Upsy-daisy now." (Who but Mattie-Miller would say upsy-daisy?)

But there was only one thing I cared about. Was my right hand all right? My knees throbbed and my left knuckles were skinned, but that was okay. As long as it wasn't my right hand. Good hand—good friend. That's all that mattered. That and the head and whatever it is that tied it all together. Head bone's connected to the hand bone. Dem bones, dem bones.

I eased my weight onto my other elbow and looked down at my right arm. I moved the fingers one at a time, like some slow-motion piano scale. Okay so far. I moved the wrist, the elbow, then carefully, carefully, the whole thing from the shoulder.

All this time Julie was kneeling there beside me saying, "Don't move. Lie still for a few minutes and take it easy."

I wanted to yell back at her, "I have to move it—see

if it *does* move. Because it's my painting arm. Don't you understand anything?"

"Sorry," I said instead. "All this fuss—feel such a fool—a break in the sidewalk—" I was fairly sputtering as I latched on to that last. "I tripped, that's all."

"The way the tree roots push these sidewalks up is a disgrace. Someone ought to call the city." This from Ernestus Stokes.

"Now we'll just get her along inside."

Her? What her? Which her? Me. "No—quite all right. I can manage on my own."

"Don't be silly. We wouldn't think of it."

"Come along, Miss Tegges. We'll just give you a hand."

"If someone ran ahead and got her bed ready, it would help."

Ready for what? "No. Not to bed. I can manage fine. Really now— No. I won't hear of it."

Then Julie was there again. "Please, Miss Tegges. Just let us help you inside. I'm a nurse and I'd feel better with you safely in your house. That was a bad fall."

Someone had me by the arm and I felt myself being rearranged, gathered up, and finally hoisted. I felt a firm hand. The butcher Norton's hand. And me a vegetarian.

Then, forming into a terrifyingly silly procession, the whole of Butternut Street invaded my house.

They were all there (except Mr. Bigelow, who had deserted during the first lull in the madness). Julie,

Slug, and David, looking edgy. Ernestus Stokes, Marian Norton, and her husband, Tom, as bland as rice pudding. Mattie-Miller.

They moved as if they had been choreographed—back and forth over my fine Spanish rug, muting its blues and reds and yellows. Circling through the living part of the house—white walls and clear wooden surfaces, books lined on shelves. Breaking out into the studio, then pulling back as if they had opened a bathroom door without knocking. They clucked, individually and in concert, about tea and rest and how a daybed was not a proper bed at all. Get out. Get out.

Suddenly I remembered the sketches pinned to the screen. My eyes flew open.

"Oh, look, she's awake now," a voice said. Fool. As if I could have slept.

"I'll get her something to drink."

"Better let her rest."

Someone put a glass of water down on a book of Rembrandt's paintings on the bedside table; set it right on a self-portrait, circling his upper face and turning it into a kind of bull's-eye. Meanwhile, the dance was still going on and I turned as each one moved past the sketches, stepping around the screen, looking at the drawings with gulps and glances. Tom Norton stopped, moved back with his hands on his hips, then inched forward again. His petunia wife came and stood beside him, reaching one silly finger out as if to touch it.

"No—" I shot up so quickly that the room spun

around me. "No—need for you all to do any more. I'm fine. Fine. And thank you so much."

They've gone. Finally. Every last one of them. Gone with their cold cloths and pillow fluffings. Their figurative jugs of chicken soup—jugs of figurative chicken soup? Whichever. And good riddance to the lot.

Picked you up, didn't they? Lying there like a great beached whale.

Pissants. I could have done it myself.

Aren't we the self-sufficient one.

Indeed.

And now talking to yourself.

So?

That doesn't augur well for your mental health.

What if I *am* talking to myself—at least I'm answering back. Oh my, that did drive Mama right up the wall—the answering back. Funny how it was only I who did it. The boys never did—Francis, Edwin, and John.

Well, my girl. Maybe you *have* gone round the bend.

No. It's just the inner voice, like the inner eye or whatever it is that's kept me going all these years. Made me into what I am. Plain and simple—all there is to it and never time to be chick or child. Or anything else for that matter.

I am a bitch. And I know it. They came in here like so many Good Samaritans hauling the beached whale between them. Set me up with pillows and drinks of water, and no sooner was the last one out the door than I was going gimp-legged around the room fanning at the after-smell of Cashmere Bouquet talcum and Coty's Muguet des bois.

I pulled a high stool over and sat in front of the screen, looking at what they had looked at but not seen. Sketches. Studies actually, for a painting that had not come together yet. But the houses were there. My big back doors. Rooftops. Porch spindles. Steps. And bits of the people, too. The mailman in an elongated letter shaped like a kite. The pattern of Mr. Bigelow's zinnias. Abstracts of Mattie-Miller's dogs. David's car in pieces on the sidewalk. The butcher's knives and a string of sausages. Marian's washing hung all in a row. Ernestus Stokes seen as a metronome. And Julie as a bird. A suggestion of the streambed was there, too, and the hill going up and down.

I turned away for a minute, rubbing at my knee and wondering what I would do tomorrow if they all came clacking around to see how I was.

"They wouldn't dare," I said out loud. "They never have—in all the years I've been here."

Yes, my lady, I thought. But today you blew it all by falling on your face. Bad show, that.

Slug

WHEN JULIE and I got back to her house it felt warm and stuffy, but that was okay, because it gave us something to do. For the next few minutes we opened windows, picked up newspapers, and put lunch dishes in the sink.

"I had hoped the storm would cool things off," Julie said, fanning herself with a dishtowel. "That's what I like about this place—it never gets really hot. With the trees, and the stream at the foot of the hill. It's almost like being in the country but it's close to downtown. Even on the hottest night . . ."

Shut up, I thought.

"Never been any need of an air conditioner. Maybe a fan if we've been having a heat wave but . . ."

I turned and went out onto the porch, with Julie following along behind me, still talking about air currents and cross ventilation. And window shades, for crying out loud. It's odd but of all the things I'd ever thought about my mother, her being a talker wasn't one of them. Why should she be? I mean, I'm not, and neither was Gussie. Sometimes Gussie and I could go for ages without saying anything at all, and when we finally did talk, the words seemed to tumble around us.

The thing I think is that you have to know someone pretty well *not* to talk to her, or have her *not* talk to you. I didn't know Julie that well.

I missed Gussie and that feeling of missing her seemed like one too many things in a day that was about ready to explode. There had been the bus trip from Virginia to Maryland; to this house and this mother; the storm and that weird procession of neighbors carrying the other one—the old woman—inside; and the odd way being in her house made me feel at home.

Harper Tegges wasn't anything like Gussie, but she reminded me of her.

"There are so many things I want to do to this house . . . so many things it needs . . . and I thought that after school was out and I'm home all day we could . . ."

I put up my hands to protect myself from Julie's words. I turned to face her, saying, "What's she like —the woman across the street?"

"Well, famous they say. Every once in a while there's a story in the paper about her—about her work at least."

"But what's she *like*?"

"Oh, I don't know *that*. I don't guess anyone else around here does, either. She's a bit eccentric. You know, there's something we could start on right away

—today," and Julie disappeared inside while I stood leaning on the rail and staring at the house across the street.

I thought about Gussie, my grandmother, and how she had been what people called eccentric, especially when she went up and down the streets gathering things out of trash cans just because she liked the way they looked; and about Miss Tegges, who painted pictures that hung in museums; and how, in a funny sort of way, that seemed to lump them together in my mind. That and the fact that they were both old—at least judging by things like gray hair and wrinkles and hands that were strong and ropy both at the same time.

Then Julie came out and handed me a piece of sandpaper.

Julie

"WELL, THE place isn't exactly House Beautiful, but I'm working on it. A windowsill a weekend—whether it needs it or not. Anyway, I've been meaning to start in on this swing and now's as good a time as any." I held up two pieces of sandpaper, handed one to Slug, and then moved around in back of the swing, bracing it against my hip.

I concentrated on one spot, rubbing it over and over until I could almost feel it growing warm beneath my hand. Dust and flecks of paint flew up around me, and I turned my head to take a breath. After a while I felt Slug lean against the other side of the swing and heard a scratching sound as she started to work.

Is this day ever going to end, I wondered, folding the sandpaper over and feeling the new part bite into the wood. It's been going on forever. She's *been here* for-ever and it's less than twelve hours since that bus pulled in. I looked at Slug, but she had her head down, concentrating on what she was doing.

The storm helped, I thought. Gave us something

to do. Even that bit with Harper Tegges was a diversion. Oh, God, what a rotten thing to think, and anyway, what am I going to dig up for tomorrow?

"You know something," I said, running my fingers along the slat of wood that I had sanded smooth. "This swing is one of the things that made me take this house in the first place. Kind of silly, isn't it? I mean, as long as there's a porch, you can go out and *buy* a swing. That and the location and the fact that it's almost never really hot—too hot— But it's a bitch in winter. Snow and ice and . . ."

Why don't you keep quiet, I told myself. But I kept on—about hot and cold and swings and how the house was such a mess when all the week before I'd practically broken my back getting it in shape. My mother would've called me a blatherskite. Gussie hated a blatherskite.

Late in the afternoon I went to get carryout for our supper. It seemed easier somehow than sitting face to face on opposite sides of the kitchen table.

We ate as we worked, sanding and wiping at the swing until it got so dark we couldn't see what we were doing and the fireflies were out and pieces of soft worn sandpaper were heaped in the open box along with pizza crusts and bunched-up paper napkins.

Harper

I woke the next morning with a headache. I hadn't slept well—my head felt worse when I was lying down —and there was a rushing feeling inside of me as if I were in a car going relentlessly from throughway to throughway. Up ramp and down ramp. Chasing, or being chased, I wasn't sure which.

Early morning has always been my favorite time of day. There is usually no one around, and when I take the dog out I walk along touching tree trunks and overhanging branches and studying the fronts of the houses that, in the half-light, look as defenseless as the faces of people sleeping in railway stations.

But this morning my house was under siege. There was a creature perched on the corner of the porch—all curlicues of fake black poodle fur, black bead eyes, and a red felt tongue to which a message was fastened with a straight pin. I leaned forward until the words swam into focus: "This cunning pooch has come to say, Have a bright and cheerful day." Signed: M-M.

I'd like to be able to vomit at will.

It looked for all the world like a grotesque I'd seen once in a bathroom never revisited. A crocheted dog whose body somehow—and for some reason—fit over an extra roll of toilet paper.

Ginger was down on the grass, barking at me to take her for a walk. We started up the hill, past the Nortons' house and David's car, with all its parts tucked neatly inside. I stopped there. The fact was I didn't trust myself to go on past Mattie-Miller's front yard, with its plaster dwarfs, gnomes, and flat-footed animals. One look at an impudent chipmunk and I'd have ground it into the dirt.

We went back down the hill and up onto the porch, where I speared the crocheted dog with the end of my stick, carried it inside, and dropped it into the kitchen trash can.

No sooner had I settled down to breakfast than I was up again, moving around the studio, unpinning the sketches from the screen, and piling them on my worktable. I threw open the double doors at the end of the room and let the light pour in. As I went to pick up an easel, to move it out of the way, it blurred before me and seemed to lunge just out of reach.

And for a minute I froze: afraid to move, afraid not to move. Then, catching hold of the edge of the table, I worked my way back to the stove, where I took a mouthful of tea. It was cold and I spit it in the sink. Then carefully, step by step, I made another cup, telling myself all the while that there was nothing wrong.

I took out the tea bag and blew the steam away, making ripples on the surface. "Ladies don't blow on their soup . . . their tea . . . their cocoa . . ." Mama used to say. "I do," I always said back to her. "I do."

I swallowed and felt it burning inside me. More. And more. Until the mug was only half full.

Slowly I started to turn, then swung around as if to catch the easel unaware. It stood there, dark brown and worn, in the morning sunlight. Its lines were sharp and unfuzzed—the upright and the wings, the canvas holders, the crank. Still holding the mug, I moved toward it, reaching for paper and pencil.

The telephone rang.

The voice, when I answered it, filled the room, booming out the open doors and into the yard. Ernestus Stokes was on the phone, and for a minute I imagined her great thundering voice pushing through her open window and down the street, meeting with the selfsame voice that had come through my phone, and was on its way up.

Because of this I missed what she was saying and had to ask her to repeat it.

"How are you feeling this morning? Better, I hope, though a little stiff, I'd venture. I've already called the city about those sidewalks and they said they'd take care of it. Probably the best thing for you today is rest. After all, it's not as if you had anything that had to be done."

I hung up the phone.

But the mood was gone and I had to work at getting it back. I sharpened pencil after pencil, gouging at them with a knife and watching the shavings drift down into the trash. I riffled through the sketches on my table. Finally I fastened a sheet of paper onto a drawing board and put it on the easel, sniffing at its clean newness. And I was frozen there, held by whatever feeling takes hold of me when I stand before an empty paper or canvas—until I make the first mark.

I started to draw, tentatively at first, trying to bring all the sketches heaped in front of me into a whole. It was as if my hand took over. There were doors in the foreground and I built them up in tones, switching then to the background, working all over the page. I changed pencils—this one, that one. I erased, sweeping at rubber dust with a feather.

There was sweat on my face; I wiped it away with my left hand. The muscles at the back of my neck screamed and I rolled my head forward, then back again. My shoulders ached, and my legs, my feet. Kicking off my sandals, I rubbed one foot against the smooth wooden floor. Still the drawing continued to grow.

I worked until I couldn't work anymore, then sat staring at the easel.

"Excuse me, Miss Tegges, I didn't want to disturb you, but I was wondering if you were all right—after your fall, I mean."

I blinked at the girl in the doorway, trying to figure out who she was and how long she had been there; trying to force myself out of the picture propped in front of me. I moved over to the sink and turned on the cold water, submerging my face in it and gulping it down as if in those hours, days, years since breakfast I had dehydrated.

The girl Slug, from across the street, I thought as I turned to see her edging her way into the room.

"I told Julie I'd come over and check on you, but I just woke up. Back home, with Gussie, we were always up early. There was always something to do—"

Christ. She wanted to talk.

"Now that I'm here—with Julie—I don't— Ever since Gussie—"

"I'm fine, really fine," I said, wiping my face with a paper towel and watching her inch closer to the easel. I wanted to run at her, to push her away.

"I don't understand it," she said, looking at the drawing. "But I like it anyway."

Did I ask you? I said to myself, feeling oddly defensive.

"I see a bird—and is that a girl, over to the side?" she asked.

"There isn't any girl," I said. "And now I have to get back to work."

"That's what my Uncle Brian always says—'Now I have to get back to work.' He's an artist too, so maybe you've heard of him. He has exhibits from time to time, and Gussie and I used to gather things for his collages."

"I really don't think so," I said. "These days anyone with a paint-by-number kit fancies himself an artist."

And she was gone.

I wanted to call her back; to let her tell me about Gussie, and Brian, her uncle, and any other thing she had to tell.

But I didn't.

Instead, I moved to stand where she had stood, to see what she had seen. There was something—a suggestion—and it could have been a girl, facing away from me. But I didn't remember putting her there and she seemed to upset the balance of things. I pulled the paper off the easel and tore it in two.

And suddenly I felt drained, as if all the strength had gone out of me and into the picture that wasn't what I wanted it to be. I lay down flat on the floor, exhausted with what I had done but strangely buoyed by what I wanted to do tomorrow.

My muscles started to unknot, my thoughts to wander. What was it the girl had said about her uncle? Brian, she said his name was. How she and someone named Gussie gathered things for his collages. I started to get up, to go to the shelf and root through the stack of *Art in America*. Then I didn't bother. I knew it was there, in an issue a while back. A cover story. Brian Wilgus. Julie's name was Wilgus.

Paint by number indeed.

And who would think he would have a sister and a niece right here on Butternut Street.

Damn.

The next morning I was back at the easel. The day, if anything, was hotter than the one before, but everything else was the same—the sheet of white paper, the sense of urgency, and especially the headache. As if everything inside my head might at any minute come spewing forth.

The lines sprawling across the page were blurred and somehow fainter than I wanted them to be. I switched to a softer pencil, using more pressure. But still the strokes seemed indefinite.

I thought of what I was working on as a street scene —of Butternut Street—and saw, in my mind's eye, the way it had to be.

Holding my arm straight out, I clenched my fingers and watched the muscles tighten and relax, tighten again. I pulled the paper off the drawing board and let it slide onto the floor as I fastened another one in its place.

Better. The lines seemed stronger now, darker and more fluid. I stopped and leaned forward, reaching out to run my finger along the shadow of a girl, her back to me. The same one that had been in the drawing the day before. And there were other things, too, pushing in from other times and other places.

I replaced the paper and began again.

And again. And again. Until the papers lay like giant playing cards around the base of the easel and the empty drawing board stared back at me.

My mouth was dry and I felt lightheaded. Had I eaten breakfast? Of course, it would be automatic—strong black tea and a roll—like walking Ginger or brushing my teeth. I looked for my mug and found it in the cupboard where I had put it the night before. While I waited for the water to boil, I kept my back to the studio as if afraid that all my failed drawings might rise up as one and thumb their noses at me.

When the water was ready I filled the mug, holding it close to my chest to ward off a chill, though the day was hot and my shirt stuck to the middle of my back. As I moved into the studio, I pushed a rocking chair over to where I had been working and sat down. For a moment I stared at the papers and the empty easel; then I put my head back, rocking from time to time. The tea, untouched, was on the floor beside me.

Faces swam at me like blowfish coming up from the sea: Mama, Papa, and my brothers. Richard and Suzanne. Suzanne, with her back to me, facing away.

I jumped up and moved across the studio, sidestepping tables heaped with palettes, paints, cans of turpentine, and brushes sticking out of jars like porcupine quills. I pulled a stack of canvases away from the wall, flipping through them until I found the one I was looking for.

I dragged it out and up onto the easel, the long way across. Stepping back, I held my hand out from my forehead to bring it into perspective; to see on the canvas what I had seen before. Then I took up a piece of charcoal and began laying in figures and shapes. The suggestion of the girl was there again, to the side of the canvas, and this time I let her stay.

I worked frantically. Feverishly. Until it was as if the studio couldn't contain me anymore. And I was through the wide-open doors and out onto the grass, swaying at first, then dancing to music from the radio propped in the kitchen window of the house next door.

I slowed, moving rhythmically, my arms outflung as if only by reaching for all outdoors could I accommodate the excitement growing inside of me. Once before I had danced like this. We were in Washington then, Richard and I. There was a pasture by the side of the house and beyond that the woods—hawthorns, alders, and a ridge of firs. It was the day we learned about the baby. I did not know yet that one kind of creativity would rob another.

"Stop it, Harper," Richard had said. "You must stop it. This dancing. This—this abandonment. It isn't seemly. It isn't— And besides, you'll harm yourself, the baby . . ."

I looked at him and knew he would never understand that on this day of all days there was nothing that could harm me or our child.

"Dance with me, Richard," I had said, pulling at his arms. "Dance."

"Stop it, Harper," he said.

And I stopped. Because I hadn't learned that I could have not stopped.

I was hungry and the cupboard was bare. " 'Old Mother Hubbard went to the cupboard . . .' " I said to Ginger.

" 'To get her poor dog a bone . . .' " I said, poking in the refrigerator at an empty milk carton and dropping a withered orange in the trash.

" 'And when she got there . . .' "

I needed food, and air, and exercise. Needed to fill myself with all those things, store them away so that I could get back to work on my painting. So that I could continue working. On and on and on.

"Not this trip, Ginger," I said to the dog as I gathered my shoes and my wallet. "I have to hurry, so I can get on with it."

But once I was out on the street I didn't hurry. I dawdled, as Mama used to say, looking up at the sky —a sharp, clear blue with the pine trees dark against it—and down at the sidewalk. I nodded to Marian Norton's petunias and to one of Mattie-Miller's dogs and thought briefly of the crocheted monstrosity still in my kitchen trash can. I waved to the mailman, waited as he crossed the street, and stood there while he prattled on about this one and that one. Up on the avenue I skimmed along, still buoyed by the excitement of the painting inside me, pushing to get out. Into the market, up and down the aisles gathering milk and fruit and cereal; dog food and a can of tuna fish. Eggs and bread. I went back outside, nodding to strangers, wanting to grab at them and say, "Wait until you see—you *will* see—what I am going to do."

When I crossed onto the last block of Butternut Street, I came upon Slug sitting on the curb with her feet pushed into a pile of seedpods, as if she was waiting for someone.

"Good morning, good morning," I said, stopping and looking down at her. "It isn't really, though, is it? The morning got away from me. Like that—" I snapped my fingers in a way that verged on the theatrical. "The work was going well and I was so caught up in it."

"There's something I've been thinking, Miss Tegges," she said, getting up quickly and looking down at me. "You *ought* to know who Brian Wilgus is. Because he's good. Because he's . . ."

"You know that, do you? For a fact?" I said, shifting the grocery bag from one arm to the other.

She looked at me for a minute, jutted her chin forward and said, "I know that for a fact. Gussie told me so. And I'll bet you something else—if you looked in

those books and magazines of yours you'd find out."
Then she reached for my bag, saying, "Here, let me
help you with that."

"No need," I said, swooshing my stick at the air
between us. "I can manage on my own. Always have."
And I turned away from her so that for a few minutes
we walked together but on opposite sides of the street.

Back in the house the excitement I had felt earlier
seemed to ooze out of me. I was drained and slightly
nauseous. After putting the groceries away, I fixed myself a plate of fruit and cheese and sat for a while,
poking at it. The cheese had a warm and somewhat
mealy taste, and I watched a slice of apple turn brown
before my eyes. Still life with grunge, I thought.

The headache was back. I looked up at the painting,
trying to see where Slug October would fit into it. I got
up and was moving toward the easel when it lurched
and I grabbed for the back of a chair.

It lurched? I lurched?

My hands felt clammy and seemed to slip against
the wood. Working my way around to the front of the
chair, I sat down, closing my eyes, opening them slowly
to see what the room was doing all around me. My
heart thumped inside my chest and I was afraid.

I saw Julie Wilgus's shadow before I saw her. It fell
across the doorway at the back of the studio, stretching long and spindly, so that I had time to rearrange
myself before she was standing in the door.

"Miss Tegges? I hope I'm not interrupting your work, but I wanted to see how you were. I'm sorry I didn't get over sooner. How *are* you?"

What I wanted to say flat out was that I was scared as hell. What I wanted to say was that there were things that blurred in front of me, that lurched at me, and at times took hold of my body like so many demon spirits and made it do or not do things.

"Fine," I said. "I put in a long, full morning—one of those times when I'm completely caught up in what I'm doing. When I stopped and came back to the real world, I had to rush out to the store. I was just sitting here catching my breath before I get back to work. Come in, why don't you."

"It's hard work, isn't it? 'Like digging a ditch,' my brother always said. He's an artist, too."

"Ye-es," I said, moving my head slightly to see what would happen and thinking that it was oddly comforting to have her here. "I didn't realize that Brian Wilgus was your brother until your daughter told me so. His collages are outstanding—a fine use of textures."

"Slug told you about Brian?" I watched Julie step around an easel almost without looking at it, as if she knew the difference between an atelier and a gallery. I liked that in her. "Well, I guess I'm not surprised," she went on. "Slug's crazy about him. And he's been good to her."

"She stopped over yesterday and I'm afraid I was pretty rude, but sometimes I get so wrapped up in what I'm doing. Anyway, I sent her scurrying—but she lived to fight another day."

"Slug did?" asked Julie, sitting down on the edge of a stool.

"She reminds me of myself at that age—what is she, about seventeen?"

"Yes—seventeen."

"That's just the age I was when I told them at home that it would be art school or nothing." And for a minute the same feeling of power washed over me that I had felt the day I confronted Mama and Papa across the dining-room table. "I suspect that daughter of yours is a tough one. Am I right?" All the while I was pushing with one foot and then the other, rocking the chair and testing the strength in my legs, wondering if when I stood up I could make it across the room without looking like a drunken reveler.

"I don't know," Julie said.

There was something about the way she said it that made me turn and look at her.

"Yes, I guess it's hard—dealing with young people today." And I suddenly thought that I was acting interested just to keep her there—that maybe the loner was suddenly afraid of being alone.

"You don't understand." She leaned toward me so that I had to catch myself to keep from pushing my chair backward, away from her. "Miss Tegges—"

"Harper."

"Harper, you don't really understand. Up until

recently—for all those seventeen years—I had never seen Slug. I don't know her at all."

You walked into that, I thought to myself. It's what you get for making clucking noises just to keep her here. And now she'll expect you to say something.

Say you don't give a damn. Say you have a painting to get on with—and a body that's obviously fighting you. Pull yourself together and say anything, as long as it gets rid of her.

"And now," I said, with the part of me that wanted to keep Julie Wilgus there obviously winning out, "you don't know how you feel."

"Yes, that's it. I don't." She got up quickly and moved back and forth. "I have to get back—there's something I have to do. Anyway, I shouldn't have mentioned it. And I'm glad to see that you're all right now, with no serious aftereffects from your fall. If there's ever anything I can do, you just be sure and let me know. We're over there—Slug and I."

And Julie was gone, leaving me as tired as I was before, but now with this awkward confidence that she had thrust upon me. That I didn't want at all. That crowded me.

For the next few days I slipped into a pattern: I got up in the morning and went to bed at night. In between I worked, and walked the dog and ate. I guess I ate, because the food in the refrigerator disappeared. I don't remember. The mail came and I brought it in, set it aside. Julie came again, stood at the back door, and went away. And after she had left, the place where she had stood blurred before me and I had to rest. Then I began again.

The painting drove me. Demanded things of me. And the work was drudging and unsparing.

And it was good.

One morning I woke earlier than usual, looked at the painting, and wasn't sure what I wanted to do.

I felt quivery on the inside, as if all the parts of me that had been held together had become unattached. I made a cup of tea and my hand shook so that I sloshed it onto my wrapper. I scarcely flinched as it washed onto my chest.

I was afraid of the way I felt—but there didn't seem to be anything to do about it. Maybe if I could rest. Catch up.

The dog whined to go out.

"Okay, Ginger," I said, reaching for my stick. "But not for a walk. Not today. We'll just go out in the yard, and in again."

When I opened the studio doors the sky was a luminous gold and pink, and as we started out the colors seemed to settle down around me.

Slug

I WOKE just after dawn with the feeling that my Grandmother Gussie had something to say to me.

But Gussie was dead, and I was here in a strange house, in a strange city, with a woman I didn't know.

As I looked around the room, the shadows gave way to chairs, doors, and window frames, and to Gussie's old leather suitcase, which I still hadn't unpacked, shoved under an eave. I watched the walls and the ceiling turn the color of oyster shells. Then I was out of bed and through the upstairs hall, going down the stairs. Partway there I stopped, as if an invisible wire had reached out to trip me, and put my foot carefully on the step. I was conscious of Julie asleep in her room. That was one thing about Gussie: we never tiptoed around each other. Somehow, through the years, the noises we made became a part of us, so that we hardly noticed them.

I threw open the front door and went outside, moving just to the edge of the porch, then back, settling into the wooden swing. The air was cool and slightly clammy, and a mist hung over Butternut Street, making the houses, and even the streambed, seem distant and somehow smudged. I poked at a paint blister on the arm of the swing, feeling it squish, and smeared a blob of wet green paint across the bottom of my foot. The slats of the seat were tacky and I wondered if when I stood up my red-and-white-striped night shirt would be crisscrossed with lines of green. Like some giant tic-tac-toe.

I reached down with one foot and pushed against the floor, making the swing rock crazily back and forth. Pulling my knees up under my chin, I thought of all the years I had waited for Julie to come; the questions I had asked Gussie that she couldn't answer; the dreams I had dreamed. Now here I was: in Julie's house. And I wasn't sure I wanted to be here.

Across the street a dog barked.

As I set the swing in motion again I held my hair, still braided from the day before, away from my back, letting wisps of cool air wrap around me.

The dog barked again. Louder this time.

I remembered how in grade school one day I had wished right out loud for Julie to come back, and how Gussie finally said she wasn't going to come. How it would go on being just the two of us. The way it had always been ever since the day Julie had hopped the Trailways bus out of town.

I jolted the swing to a stop with my feet, so that it threw me against the back and made my legs tremble.

I got up and went to the porch steps, then down onto the walk.

The small red dog with the curling tail, Miss Tegges's dog, was running up and down the street. She barked, stopped to look around, and barked again. When she saw me she ran over, pawed at my legs, and backed away, as if trying to tell me something.

"What is it, dog? What're you doing out here?"

When the dog turned and started toward the yellow house, I followed.

Miss Tegges was lying on the ground just outside the studio doors. Her eyes were partway open, with only a rim of white showing between the lids, and her breath seemed to come in patches.

I moved closer and stood over her, waiting to make sure she was really breathing before I turned and ran— back across the street and through the house. Up the stairs.

And then Julie was awake, asking me questions and making some kind of sense out of the answers I managed to give her.

"Okay," she said, turning me toward the steps. "You go back and stay with her. I'll throw on some clothes and come right along."

I can't, I thought, as I went back down the steps and across the street. "I just *can't*," I said out loud. I felt as if I had done all this before; pictures of Miss Tegges and Gussie swirled together in my mind.

When I got there, Miss Tegges was still crumpled on the grass, her face the color of bone, one arm flung up over her head. The dog crouched beside her and whined, her cry rising above all the morning noises up and down the street.

"Julie's coming, Miss Tegges. Can you hear me? She's on her way," I said, digging my fingernails into the palms of my hands and looking over my shoulder to see if she really was coming.

And then Julie was there. She knelt beside Miss Tegges, feeling for a pulse, lifting her eyelids. Stepping over her, she moved into the studio, and I wanted to follow her, to keep her always between me and the woman sprawled like some grotesque rag doll outside.

"I've called for an ambulance," she said when she came back out. She settled down on the grass next to Miss Tegges's head, wiping a trace of spittle away from her mouth, taking her hand.

"What is it, do you think?" I asked, swallowing back the feeling that I wanted to turn and run.

"I don't know," said Julie. "She could have fallen and knocked herself out. But I'm afraid there's more. Why don't you go over and get dressed. Come back when you're ready. Okay?"

That was all it took and I was gone. Running. Feeling suddenly free. Upstairs I stepped into the shower, not even waiting for the water to warm up. I unfastened the braid and let my hair hang loose, and felt it grow wet and heavy against my back. I dried myself, wrapping the towel around my head, and walked naked into my room, leaving a pattern of splotchy footprints behind me.

I reached for a pair of pants, a skirt, and a shirt, moving over to the window and putting them on as I watched an ambulance come down the street, turn around, and pull up in front of the house across the street.

I knew that I should hurry, get back to Julie to see if there was anything I could do, but I stood where I was, rubbing my hair with a towel. My fingers seemed to move in slow motion as I pulled the brush through my hair and watched the water splatter onto my clothes and down onto the floor around me. Plucking a rubber band off one of the bedposts, I fastened it around the hair I had pulled back away from my face. I dug a pair of sandals out from under the bed and went back to the window, watching the ambulance across the street, its red light revolving on top. The doors were open, the stretcher gone.

The ambulance had come for Gussie, too, and gone away empty again. Because Gussie had already been dead.

She had been dead when I went into her room that morning in May, wondering why the sun was so high in the sky with no sounds coming from the kitchen below—no whistle from the tea kettle or opening of a cupboard door.

Gussie had been propped up in bed, looking small against the red corduroy pillow. There was an open magazine across her lap, and the light from the bedside lamp jarred against the sunlight. I called to her, softly at first, then louder. I touched her shoulder, shaking it, thinking of nothing except that the stuffing oozing out of the seams of the pillow looked like dandelion seeds.

I could blow on it, I thought.

And make a wish.

Without feeling anything at all, I walked downstairs and called Dr. Mercy. I went back upstairs and sat next to the bed, reaching for my grandmother's hand, which was cool and oddly rigid.

They had arrived together, Dr. Mercy and the men from the rescue squad, stamping up the stairs of that scruffy little house and filling all of Gussie's room. They moved around the bed, pushing me out of the way, so that when I stepped back I hit my head against the sloping roof. And for some reason I stood there, fingering the wallpaper rather than the bump on my head. They worked over Gussie, pulling away the red corduroy pillow and throwing it onto the floor. A wisp of stuffing hovered in the air before settling on top of it. Poor dandelion, I thought. Make a wish. Make a wish. They stood back away from the bed, and one of the men (the short one with the sweat stain on the back of his shirt) turned off the lamp, leaving the room, if anything, brighter without it. They had ushered me down the stairs and into the front room.

"She didn't suffer, Slug. Gussie died peacefully sometime during the night," Dr. Mercy said after the men from the rescue squad had left with their empty ambulance. She pushed me down on the daybed and sat beside me. Her small knobby hand was somehow enormous holding on to mine, and I could feel all her toughness pouring into me. When she got up and went to the telephone, I moved over into Gussie's rocking chair and sat there stiffly while she made her calls. To Mr. Disharoon from the funeral parlor, and Brian in New York, and Henley, who was my best friend and who had lived with Dr. Mercy for the past five years.

Mr. Disharoon came first, bringing his nephew John Henry, who had been in my class at school since first grade and who acted as if he'd never seen me before. They followed Dr. Mercy up the steps and I heard them moving overhead, heard John Henry swear sharply as they seemed to scuffle at the top of the stairs. They made their way through the front room, the stretcher covered with a white sheet between them, and they had to veer around me because it didn't occur to me to move. That I could move. They kicked at the screen door so that it flopped back against the outside wall and stayed that way.

Henley came next, talking to Dr. Mercy in the kitchen, moving close to me and touching me quickly on the shoulder. "Aunt Mercy's going now—she has office hours, but she'll be back. And I'll be here, in case you want me."

I heard her there, all afternoon, pushing back and forth on that rusty old glider out on the porch, the one where we used to play Monopoly, with the board across our knees and the hundred-dollar bills stuffed down between the crackly plastic cushions. I heard it squeaking in long, painful sounds, as daylight faded and darkness settled in. Until Brian got there, all the way from New York.

The men across the street slid the stretcher into the ambulance and for a minute I caught at the window-sill, leaning forward, pressing my forehead against the glass. No, I thought, they didn't take Gussie. She was already dead. It isn't Gussie but somebody else. The woman across the street. Miss Tegges, the artist.

I turned and went downstairs, moving slowly and standing just inside the screen door until the ambulance started up the hill, its siren beginning to whine. Then I went back across the street, where I found Julie trying to keep the dog Ginger in the studio while she struggled to close the double doors.

"We'll have to do something about this dog later on," she said. "But I've given her fresh water and I guess she'll be okay for now. Let me get my keys and we'll go over to the hospital."

The feet under the curtains of the cubicle moved backward and forward. Stepping sideways. Turning. Shifting. Rocking. I concentrated on them as if they were, of themselves, important. Scuffed, or white and spanking-clean. I sat next to Julie on a straight-backed chair in the emergency room, my eyes down, as if afraid that by looking head-on at all those people pushing their way in and out of the cubicle I might become a part of that world of carts and stretchers and machines that hissed; of basins and bundles of dirty linen.

There was a jangling of curtain hooks along the rod, and a woman with a clipboard emerged, looking up and down the hall and calling, "Is there anyone here with Miss Tegges? I need some information."

"I told you there was no one" came a voice from behind the curtain. "I don't know how I got here—or why—but I can damn well tell you I didn't bring an entourage with me. I don't even *know* an entourage."

"She's conscious, then," said Julie, getting up and speaking to the woman. "How is she?"

"You'll have to speak to the doctor about that, but right now I need some information," the woman said, moving down the hall so quickly that Julie and I had to run to catch up.

"Now," she said, tapping her pencil against her

front teeth, "I've been waiting for someone from the family."

"But I'm not—we're not—family," Julie said. "We're just neighbors. My daughter was the one who found her. And I called the ambulance."

"Well, there really *should* be someone from the family here. I have forms to be filled out."

"I don't know that there *is* anyone," Julie said.

The woman seemed to sag for a minute; she tapped harder at those front teeth and said, "Oh, one of those. In that case I will have to go back in there and try to get the information from the patient myself." And she sounded just like the little red hen, the one who was always going to do everything herself.

"We'd like to see Miss Tegges now," Julie said. "To reassure her."

"Oh, I don't know about that, seeing as you're not fam-i-ly." She said the word slowly and in three syllables, in a tone that implied that both Julie and I had something to answer for.

But Julie had turned and was walking down the hall, slipping neatly through the opening in the curtain.

I waited there for a minute, the tooth-tapper on one side and the lightly stirring curtain of Miss Tegges's cubicle on the other. Then I plunged after Julie, poking at the curtains that billowed around me, trapping me. Suddenly I felt claustrophobic as I clawed at the heavy cloth, breathing in all those hospital smells that seemed to be captured there.

Miss Tegges was propped on one elbow, looking at me. Her face was slightly flushed and she wore a rumpled gown with *St. Francis Hospital* marching across a pattern of pink flowers.

"Christ," she said. "It *is* an entourage."

The woman with the clipboard pushed her way in, moving close to the stretcher.

"A multitude," Miss Tegges said, dropping back down and closing her eyes.

"Now, now, I *have* to have answers to these questions."

Miss Tegges lay immobile, her head tilted slightly back, so that for a moment I thought she had lost consciousness again.

"Now, let me see, I have your name, your address, your date of birth. I need to know your religious affiliation."

"Heathen."

"Now, now—"

"I am a heathen. H-E-A-T—"

The clipboard woman melted into the curtain and disappeared as Miss Tegges struggled up on her elbow again, clutching the sheet and turning on Julie.

"Is this your doing? Yours and—hers," she said, stabbing a finger in my direction. "Where are the rest of them—Mattie-Miller, the butcher, the baker, the candlestick maker? Then we could have a *swarm*. Entourage. Multitude. Swarm. Good, better, best. That's what Mama used to say. 'Good, better, best, never let it rest. Till the good is better, and the better best.'

"And now a *swarm*. A swarm of busy bees—busy-bodies. Good God Almighty, I've spent a lifetime wanting to be left alone." Her voice rose sharply and she turned away from us, facing into the curtains, the gown falling open so that her bare back was toward us. "I've got to get out of here. Got to get home. There are things to be done. Work. And oh, my God, my head hurts."

She lunged suddenly, throwing her legs over the side of the stretcher and sitting up, reaching for her head and tilting forward.

The cubicle filled with people. Doctors and nurses reaching for Miss Tegges, pushing her back. Talking. Soothing.

I stepped back through the opening in the curtain and pulled Julie with me. "It *is* a swarm," I said out loud.

A doctor followed us out, dropping a folder at the desk and turning to Julie. "She'll have to be admitted, be seen by a neurologist. How long has your mother had—"

I could feel Julie stiffen beside me as she said, "She's not my mother. I'm a neighbor."

"Has there been anything that you've noticed, any unsteadiness, trouble with vision? Any weakness?"

"She fell a week or so ago, but other than that—

Actually we hardly know her. She's very independent. An artist who works at home."

"There are tests that will have to be run. I'm Dr. Evans, and if you'll just get back in touch with me I hope I'll be able to tell you something more."

"But—" said Julie. "But I'm not any relation."

"Someone should keep in touch. Have me paged when you come to visit her—and leave your name and number at the desk." And he was gone, disappearing into another set of curtains as if he had been swallowed up.

"Wait—" Julie and I were almost at the door when a nurse came running up behind us saying, "The dog. Don't forget the dog. Miss Tegges said—asked—if you would please . . ."

"What she probably said, with no 'please' about it, was 'Tell those goddamn busybodies if they want to do something, to take care of the dog,' " said Julie.

"More or less," the nurse said, rolling her eyes.

"There's more?" asked Julie.

"Oh, lots—but the only thing you need to hear is 'With ice cubes.' "

"Ice cubes?" we both asked at the same time.

"Ice cubes. Ginger—the dog, I guess—needs ice cubes in her water bowl."

And I wanted out. I stepped down hard on the treadle, waiting for the door to open.

. . .

After dinner that night, when I came in from emptying the trash, Julie was sitting at the kitchen table with
a cup of tea. "This last week at school is going to be
busy, frantic actually, but if you could just manage to
entertain yourself until next Friday there will be lots
of things for us to do together."

"I want to look for a job," I said. "I mean, I have to
find one, with the whole summer ahead of me like
this."

"Oh, Slug, no. Not this summer. I thought this
would be a good chance for us to get acquainted.
There'll be plenty of time for you to get a job later on,
when you . . ."

"Get acquainted? Get acquainted?" I moved closer
to the table, looking down at Julie, thinking that she
was small the way Gussie had been small, and surprised
to remember that she was Gussie's daughter. Because
I felt oversized, I moved over to the refrigerator, pressing my back flat against it, while the word spun inside
of me. Acquainted. Acquainted. Acquainted.

"You really wanted to get acquainted, didn't you?"
I said, pushing off from the front of the refrigerator.
"All those years—and even when you came to Gussie's
funeral, hunched there like something out of a bad
movie. You would have left again, gotten on another
Trailways bus, if Brian hadn't stopped you. That's how
much you wanted to get acquainted."

And I ran through the house, out onto the porch. I

flopped down on the swing, heard the hooks squeak in the ceiling overhead, and jumped up, wiping my hands against my skirt. I moved down to the bottom step, out of the shaft of light from the open door, and sat, arms locked around my knees.

When Brian had gotten there I was still sitting in my grandmother's rocking chair; still rocking, and when I stopped, the muscles twitched inside my legs. There was a peanut-butter-and-jelly sandwich on a plate on the floor beside me and a glass of milk that had a film across the top and looked yellowish in the lamplight.

Brian had come into the house, tossing his bag on the floor. All in one gesture, he reached for me, pulling me up and steadying me as my legs shook beneath me. "Slug—Slug, I got here as soon as I could, but you just can't *get* here in a hurry. I flew into Salisbury and rented a car, but it's still forever. It's been a long time for you to be alone. I felt better after I called Dr. Mercy from the airport and she said that Henley was here with you."

I looked toward the porch, but he shook his head. "I sent her along home. Thought we could manage now."

He led me out into the room, guiding me slowly until I was moving on my own. "Now," he said, "I think you should eat something. Let's see what we can find."

I wasn't hungry, and then I was starving and ate all the scrambled eggs that he heaped on my plate. Afterward Brian put the dishes in the sink and sat down again, holding his pipe without lighting it and shaking his head back and forth. "It seems so *normal*," he said. "As if at any minute Gussie'll come down the steps and into the kitchen, wanting to know why we'd gone ahead and eaten without her." And as if we'd come too close to something we weren't ready for yet, we talked about little things: the weather, the food on the airplane, the new shopping center at the edge of town.

All of a sudden we were talking about Gussie— about her gift ("more like a curse," Gussie used to say) for seeing into the future, and the people of the town who came begging for the things they hoped she could tell them. We talked about the way she liked gewgaws—treasures, she called them—collecting bits of colored glass and stones and clock springs, storing them in bags and boxes around the house.

We talked about Gussie until long after midnight, so that by the time we went upstairs I was able to stand at the door of her room (tidied by Dr. Mercy or Henley while I rocked woodenly through the afternoon) and then move on to my own bed. And finally to sleep.

The next day I went with Brian to make the arrangements for Gussie's funeral. When we got back to the house we sat in the front room for a few minutes, looking at the collection of shells and polished stones on every tabletop, at the colored glass bottles lining the windowsills. "Gussie's treasures," Brian said, shaking a handful of marbles out of the coffee can and holding one up to the light the way Gussie used to do.

"All this probably explains why I make collages instead of paintings or prints or etchings like a sensible person. Remember, I grew up with this stuff. Same as you did."

"Same as Julie did?" I asked.

"Same as Julie did," he said, moving to stand by the window, fingering the scrap of curtain hanging there. "And now," he went on without turning around, "we have to do something with it all. With this whole place."

Even then it didn't register that it was me he was talking about. Not until he said, "You know that any other time you could have come with Leslie and me."

As if from far away I heard Brian talking about going to work in Italy for a year, subletting his apartment. And I had to scrabble to catch up.

"Listen, Brian, you don't have to worry about me. I'm okay. I can get a job and—I'll stay right here."

"You're too young."

"I'm seventeen." I turned and went into the kitchen, putting the kettle on, lighting a match, and waiting for the popping sound as the gas caught and the flame shot up.

"And anyway, this house belongs to Mr. Trimper. Gussie'd rented it for years—as long as I can remember." Brian followed me into the kitchen, taking mugs and tea bags out of the cupboard.

"I'm going to be a sort of exchange teacher in Florence for a year. And Leslie's coming with me. She can finish her book over there."

"You never brought her down here. You promised Gussie you would and you never did," I said, wondering why I suddenly wanted to hurt him.

"Don't you think I know that? Like I never told Gussie about the year in Italy, hadn't gotten around to it, because—because there was always going to be so much time. And one day there wasn't. It had all run out."

The kettle screamed and Brian yanked it off the stove. "It's just that the timing is so damn bad," he said.

"I'm sorry she inconvenienced you."

"Goddamn it, Slug. She *was* my mother," he said, slamming his hand down on the table.

And for the first time I realized that he looked the way I felt: raw-edged.

We stood on opposite sides of the kitchen table, not saying anything, until Brian picked up the kettle and poured water into the mugs. I added sugar and pushed one mug over to him.

"I'm sorry," I said.

"Don't worry," he said, reaching out to squeeze my

hand for a minute. "Something will work out. I'm sure I can find someone for you to board with in town this year. After you finish high school here you can come to New York with us. Go to college up there."

They buried Gussie in a little cemetery twenty miles up the highway, next to the grandfather I had never known.

GEORGE EDWIN WILGUS, the marker said. It was a double stone with lilies chiseled down the sides and an empty space next to my grandfather's name.

Empty for Gussie, I thought as I shifted from one foot to the other and looked at the people crowded around. They were all there: Dr. Mercy and Henley; Mrs. Lynam, who lived next door; and the neighbors up and down the street; Mr. Trimper, who owned the dry-goods store—and, it seemed, Gussie's house—and his wife; Miss Albright, who taught me in sixth grade and was now married to Jason Burton, the town policeman; the two Mr. Fitchetts from the secondhand store.

Dr. Stark's voice droned on. ". . . and take unto yourself, O Lord, our sister Emmaline Wilgus . . ."

I looked from him back to the coffin and the wildflowers heaped by the side of the grave. "Gussie," I whispered. "Gussie."

Then it was over, with everybody milling around, talking to Brian, to me, to each other. Mr. Disharoon and his nephew John Henry worked at taking down the canopy. They moved the flowers, dallying there while they waited for the crowd to disperse so they could get on with the work of lowering the casket into the grave.

Dr. Mercy was the first to leave, kissing me and moving with Henley across the stubbly grass to her car. For a minute I wondered how long it would be before Henley and I would be normal with each other again. The rest followed, in twos and threes, stopping to talk along the way, pausing at family plots to pluck weeds, to stand for a minute with heads bowed.

I felt, rather than saw, Brian break away. I turned from Mr. Trimper ("Take your time about getting out of the house," he had said. "Though guess now's the time for me to get in there and make some changes. Spruce the place up") and was alone. I saw Brian coming back toward me, and the woman standing off to the side where the cemetery came abruptly up against a field. At first I thought it was Leslie—that she had come, for Gussie. And to be here with Brian.

Then I saw Brian's face and I knew. Even before he took my hand and led me back across the grass, stepping over markers and metal flower urns. Even as Mr. Fitchett's pickup truck sputtered in the background and a crow cawed overhead. Even as I hung back, waiting for Brian to prod me along, I knew that the woman was Julie.

"Slug, here is—" Brian said.

"Yes," I said.

"Julie, this is Slug." Brian turned sideways, between the two of us.

"Mary Rose," Julie said. "I named you Mary Rose."

"Yes," I said again, wondering what else I was supposed to say.

"Now," said Brian, rubbing his hands together and dropping them quickly down by his side. "Let's—why don't we go back to the house where we can—we'll get a chance to— I mean—"

"No," Julie said. "I think I'll head on back. I just came for the service." She turned, gesturing vaguely to the car parked on the road beyond the cemetery.

"Now that you're here—have come all this way," Brian went on.

"I don't think so." Julie shifted her bag from one shoulder to the other. "I'll just—"

"At least have something to eat. People have brought all kinds of food." Brian shrugged and moved as if to rub his hands again.

"Shilly-shallying is what Gussie would have said. What you're doing now," I said out loud, as much to stop their wavering back and forth as for any other reason. And I turned and ran, without looking back, over to Brian's rented car. I got in, catching my breath at the rush of heat, slammed the door, and waited there, not saying anything until Brian came and started the engine. We waited at the gate for Julie's car before we drove down the back road, past the Exxon station and out onto the highway.

"Did you know that she . . . I mean, did you know that Julie was coming?"

"No," said Brian. "I called her from New York after Dr. Mercy called me because . . . well, because Gussie was her mother. Just so she would know. I didn't think, after all these years—"

"Seventeen years."

"After seventeen years, that she would come back."

"How did you know where to find her? Gussie always said she didn't know where Julie was."

"I didn't either, until a year ago. There was a thing in *Newsweek*, at the time of an exhibit. Julie saw it and wrote me a note, a line actually. But there was a return address. I wrote her back, that was all. I haven't heard from her since. And I never mentioned it to Gussie. Guess I figured Julie knew where Gussie was."

"Yeah," I said. I mean, what else was there *to* say?

Brian looked in the rearview mirror. "I keep thinking she'll turn off along the way. Head back where she came from. But she's still with us."

I slid down in the seat, jamming my legs against the dashboard, closing my eyes, and trying not to think about whether Julie was behind us. I stayed that way until I could tell by the way the car slowed and turned and finally stopped that we were home. Even then I waited for Brian to get out of the car and slam the door, for the sound of another car door just in back of us, before I got out.

We sat at the kitchen table eating the chicken salad and deviled eggs and pickled watermelon rind that the neighbors had left. We drank Miss Albright's lemonade and ate the brownies from Mrs. Stark. And because there were things we couldn't talk about, we talked about Brian's work, the exhibits, the year in Italy, and the course he was going to teach.

"Oh, Slug," he said, leaning forward suddenly so that the front legs of his chair hit the floor. "I've got to call Dr. Mercy and settle things about your staying with her."

"Staying—with Dr. Mercy?" Julie said, looking from one of us to the other.

"Yes, she offered. Slug would come with me to New York, but now, with Leslie and me leaving for Italy, it presents a problem."

"She could come to me." And I saw Julie bite her lip, as if surprised at the words she had spoken.

"It would just be for a year," Brian said. "Till the end of high school, and by the time she's ready for college, we'll be back and she can live with us."

I watched them arranging and rearranging parts of my life as if I weren't there.

"Yes," Julie said. "Yes. There's room. I have a place now—a little house."

"If you're sure. If you *could*, I'd feel better about it. It was good of Dr. Mercy to offer, but—"

"Brian, I *could*. I *can*. I couldn't then but I can now."

"There'll be some money. Gussie's money that she saved from the pension. Not much, but it *is* for Slug. And anything here that she wants."

"*She* is the cat," I said, jumping up and clattering back against the stove. "Gussie always said that." I stood there swaying, looking down at Brian, who already seemed to be a step away from me. Back in New York. On his way to Italy. And at Julie, my mother.

There was a shed at the back of Gussie's house: a place where I used to go and hide until whatever was wrong was right again. That's where I wanted to be, crouching up against the potato barrel, pulling the darkness in around me, waiting for them both to leave. Afterward I could creep out and live by myself in Gussie's house. Like one of those last-people-on-earth books filled with silence and a crashing aloneness.

"Well," said Julie, getting up quickly, "I'm going to the bathroom. You two talk. And whatever you decide—" She stood for a minute in the kitchen doorway, fingering the notches in the wood where Gussie had measured our growing up—hers, and Brian's, and lastly, mine. "It's up to you, Slug."

"It's up to you, Slug," said Brian, breaking the last brownie in half and handing me a piece. "But you always said you were waiting for Julie to come back."

And now she's here, I thought, remembering all the times I had put Julie into the rooms of Gussie's house, into my life. Moving her about like a paper doll. I stood still, listening to my mother overhead, hearing her footsteps, tentative and awkward-sounding in the empty rooms.

Julie coughed and shifted on the other end of the step, where she had come to sit. And I knew that for a while at least I had known she was there.

"I always forget that Gussie was really Emmaline," I said.

"Yes," said Julie, "except that she was always just Gussie, even when I was there. Names are funny, sort of."

"Funny how?" I asked.

"I don't know. They stick or they don't stick. And once they do, there's no shaking them. No getting back to what they might have been."

"Like Slug?"

"Like Slug." Julie reached for a firefly and missed and went on. "When you were born it was October—"

"With the roses still on the bushes," I heard myself say in a voice that sounded like an echo from another time.

"You were the prettiest baby, like a rose. And I said, 'We'll call her Mary Rose October.'"

"And Gussie said—do you *remember* what Gussie said?"

" 'She looks like a slug-a-bed—we'll call her Slug.' "

I jumped up quickly, moving away from this conversation that for a moment threatened to come too close. "I'm going over to let that dog out before I go to bed," I said as I started across the street.

"Wait," Julie said, coming to the edge of the sidewalk. "Take the key to the front door. I locked it when I went over to feed her. Oh, and Slug, I have to work tomorrow, but if you get a chance you might go and visit Miss Tegges. The bus up on the avenue'll take you right to the door of the hospital. Okay?"

I unlocked the door and went inside, catching my breath at the sudden sharp smell of turpentine and paint. I turned the light on, reaching down to pat Ginger, and stopping in front of a large painting on an easel that looked like a more finished version of the drawing Miss Tegges had been working on the last time I was here. The colors were bright and seemed to be celebrating something, which wasn't at all the way I felt. The thing was that I didn't really want to go and see her tomorrow or any other day. She was bossy and insulting, calling Brian a paint-by-number artist. And besides, I had wanted her to be like Gussie and she wasn't.

But even as I thought these things, I knew what I was going to do. Because in all my childhood fantasies I had played a game of "If" with myself. "If Julie comes back I will do anything she wants: eat my carrots or clean my room, get an A in math, grow my fingernails." "Or visit Miss Tegges," I said, reaching down and fastening the leash on to Ginger's collar.

Ginger and I started up the hill, stepping over an electric cord that stretched across the sidewalk and a collection of tools heaped there on a piece of newspaper. The Nortons' orange Pinto was parked at the curb, its hood up, with a lamp dangling over the engine. David Norton was leaning into the abyss, making a series of tapping noises, and for a minute I stopped to watch, half thinking that he was some fiendish sort of dentist at work on a wide-mouthed land monster.

"Hey, how about a torque wrench?" he said, his hand waving backward toward me.

I picked it up and put it into his hand as I said, "How about giving the patient a shot of Novocain first —surely you're not going to do an extraction without it?"

He swung around to face me, saying, "Sorry. I thought you were my father."

"That's okay. I thought you were Dr. Painless."

He started to laugh, rubbing at a spot of grease on his forehead with the back of his hand. "You know what a torque wrench is?"

"Sure."

"How?"

"Because of Gussie, my grandmother. We had an old wreck of a car once and she used to work on it herself, until the time it was so bad off even Mr. Fitz-Hugh down at the garage couldn't fix it."

"I saw you the other day—with Julie Wilgus," he said.

"She's my mother."

"Yes."

And somehow the way that yes didn't have any questions behind it made me want to fill in the blanks. "I came after my grandmother died."

"Gussie?"

"Yes, Gussie," I said.

"That's rough. I'm sorry."

"Thanks. And now I've got to finish school up here next year, and then I'm supposed to go to New York, to my Uncle Brian, for college. I don't know about that, though. I mean, by that time I won't have to go *to* anyone. I'll be able just to *be*. Don't you think?"

"You wish," he said, just as Ginger tangled herself in the yellow rubber cord and sent the light bulb bobbling back and forth. David grabbed for the lamp as I grabbed the dog and pulled her out of the way.

"Isn't that Miss Tegges's dog?" he asked.

"Yes. Did you know she is in the hospital?"

"What happened? What's the matter with her?"

"I'm not sure. I found her around back early this morning. Actually, Ginger found *me* and made me find *her*. Then Julie got an ambulance and they took her to the hospital. Now they're keeping her for tests."

"It wasn't that fall she had last week, was it? When we all went tromping through her studio. God, she must have hated that."

"I don't know, but Julie says there may be a connection. Anyway, that other time everybody was only trying to help," I said.

"Yeah, but Harper Tegges isn't one for help. She's pretty much her own person."

"I ought to tell Julie that. She thinks I should go to see her tomorrow or the day after that."

"Don't you want to?" David asked, stooping down to gather his tools.

"Oh, I don't know. She seems so—"

"Come on," David said. "She's okay. Once you get to know her."

Since I couldn't think of any reason for ever wanting to know Harper Tegges, I moved closer to the car and changed the subject. "What're you working on?"

"Nothing." For a minute he stopped as if the conversation had come to an end; then he leaned back against the side of the car and went on. "Actually, what I'm doing is thinking about my work, but if I sat on the back steps staring at the sky, my father'd have a fit. The feet sticking out from under the car—or in this case the butt from under the hood—are a kind of *trompe l'oeil.*"

"What's that?" I unhooked Ginger's leash and watched as she sniffed around the tools before settling down next to them.

"Well, literally it means 'deceives the eye.' It's a painting that creates the illusion of what's shown. You have to understand that if my father sees feet sticking out from under a car, that makes it all right. I mean, having a son who's a grease monkey is okay; having a son who's an artist is not."

"Are you an artist?"

"Someday. I'm working at it, anyway. You know, once I did a painting of feet under a car. It's sort of my logo."

"Can I see it?" I asked.

"It's not here." David unhooked the lamp from the hood and turned it off, so that for a second—before the light from the streetlights and the houses up and down the street filtered in—we were in total darkness. "It's with all my other stuff, at the place where I do my work."

"You have your own studio?" I asked.

"Not exactly," he said.

I was beginning to feel like a bumper car, coming up short and changing direction. "How can you work on cars if you don't like it?" I asked.

"The funny thing is, I do," said David, going around to lower the hood. "There was some pretty heavy stuff going on between me and my father about five years ago, and something was wrong with the Pinto at the time, and well, you know the drill, any self-respecting American—pronounce that *Amurican*—boy'd be able to set it right. I was so damn mad I went at the car with a monkey wrench. The weird thing was that it all started to make sense, so I went to the library and got a book—something like *The Care and Feeding of Your Pinto*—came back, and started taking the car apart, putting it bit by bit into shoeboxes I'd scrounged up around the house, labeling the boxes. When my father came home he got into it with me, and together we rebuilt the whole thing. I had taken that miserable car apart and put it back together again before I was old enough to get a driver's license. Anyway, it was something. Look, it's the only thing my father and I can talk about without biting each other's head off. The one and only thing."

"Don't knock it," I said, looking over toward Julie's house without meaning to. "One thing isn't all bad. Anyway, with you interested in art, it must be terrific having Miss Tegges right next door. I mean, if she's as good . . ." My words sputtered and faded away because of the way David was looking at me.

"Forget it," he said. "If you've got any ideas about the famous artist taking on the guy next door as a protégé, forget it. That's not her style. And she does have style. Go visit her in the hospital and you'll find out. And by the way, ask her if I can come see her in a few days." He picked up the lamp and followed the extension cord back through the bushes in front of the house, saying, "I've got to be someplace now, but I'll see you around. Okay?"

"Okay," I said as I followed Ginger up the sidewalk.

. . .

When I got to the hospital the next day, the room was empty and the nurse at the desk said that Miss Tegges had been sent down for an electroencephalogram.

"Oh," I said, eyeing the elevator and hoping that I could time my bolt across the floor with the opening of its doors, like a well-planned escape. "Well then, I'll come another time." I started to move backward and collided with a gift cart, being pushed by a volunteer in a yellow smock, sending tins of talcum powder and assorted toy cars tumbling down around us both. I crawled around on the floor retrieving them, piling them higgledy-piggledy on top of the magazines, and watching as the elevator door slid shut.

"Oh, you're here to see Miss Tegges, aren't you?" said the nurse, peering down at me over the counter. "Why don't you go on down to her room. They should be sending her back up soon."

And I found myself waiting in a room that was more deserted somehow than just a room without people in it ought to be. I stood at the window staring down, then looked at the tightly made bed and the empty drinking glass with a skin of plastic pulled across the top. I folded my arms and leaned on the tray table, rolling it back and forth, imagining myself taking off on it down the hall, scooting around corners and through doorways. When I looked down I was surprised to see that I had gathered together a small pile of papers, folding them lengthwise and fluting the edges.

I straightened up and fanned the papers out on the table in front of me. The writing was bold and heavy, so that the wavers in it were all the more noticeable. I read one, and wished that I hadn't. I read another: "The night seemed to last forever . . ." "Just lying there in pain—and my mind going round in circles . . ."

I seemed to hear Miss Tegges's voice as I flipped a page over and read: "I'm not used to being sick and sure don't like being incapacitated. It's *hell*."

There was a heading, "People to get in touch with" —and underneath it the name "Julie Wilgus." There was something kind of sad about that. I mean, as far as I could tell, Miss Tegges scarcely even *knew* Julie. Suddenly I felt as though I had just walked through a cold mist, and I looked over my shoulder as I shuffled the rest of the papers.

"Dear Richard . . ." was at the top of a page, the letters traced over and over so that the words took on a stubborn, stocky look. There were numbers that drifted off the side of the paper and the name "Suzanne" scrawled from top to bottom, then written again, the letters spaced far apart so that only up to the "A" was repeated there. There was a list with items jumbled to one side, so that I had to work to sort them out: "paper —pencils—extra glasses—books—Good Christ, something for my head—"

When I heard voices in the hall I pushed away and

sent the table sliding along the bed, as the papers fluttered to the floor. By the time the door swung open, I was standing at the window, looking out. I turned as an aide pushed Miss Tegges into the room.

"You're back," Miss Tegges said, as if I had just gone down the hall to the water fountain. She didn't say any more until she was in bed and the aide had poured her a glass of ice water and picked up the papers from the floor, piling them on the table again.

"That's good, because there are things I need." Miss Tegges seemed to be looking at a spot just to my left side, and I shifted slightly into her line of vision, watching her eyes come slowly into focus.

"How's Ginger? Did they tell you about the ice cubes? Is she—"

"I take her out, and Julie feeds her after work. I saw David Norton and he asked for you."

"Yes," she said.

"And that woman with the dogs and the funny red hair."

"Dyed."

"Well, I don't know, but—"

"It is. Mattie-Miller, who works at the Toadvine Veterinary Clinic."

"She said to tell you—"

"Yes indeedy," said Miss Tegges in a mincing voice. "Yes indeedy, upsy-daisy and deedy-do. Is that what she said?" She made as if to spit, and rubbed her left hand up and down the side of her leg.

"It's like being in prison. Yesterday—and the day before. They take things out—blood, piss, anything they can get. They put things in, too, but the replacements aren't— They're getting more than they give."

"I'm sorry," I said. "Are you feeling better?"

"Like shit. They haven't wanted that yet, but who knows. Now, I want you to bring me a few things from the house." She waved her hand, saying, "There's paper somewhere that I borrowed from one of the nurses. Write them down."

And I jumped as if I'd been burned, moving to the other side of the bed and thinking how I wanted to tell Miss Tegges to stop giving orders. How it was only because of Julie that I had come to visit her at all. If David Norton thought *she* was so terrific, there must be something wrong with *him.* "That's okay," I said. "I don't need the paper. I'll remember."

"Paper and pencils, one of the sketch pads on my desk, but not too large a one. Extra glasses, these are blurry and things look funny. And a couple of books from the bookcase by the front door. Do you have any idea what is on the library cart somebody trundles in and out of here? *Romances*, that's what. Ro . . ."

The voice faded out, the hand stopped moving, and she was asleep.

I went back at lunchtime the next day, carrying a covered custard cup along with Miss Tegges's things in a brown paper bag.

"What's that, tea and sympathy?" she asked, pushing at the table in front of her.

"Baked custard. From Ernestus Stokes. She says hello."

"Hello, herself. And disgusting—to the custard."

"I brought this all the way down here," I said, moving the tray to one end of the table and piling the sketch pad and pencils and books on the other.

"You eat it, then," Miss Tegges said, waving a soup spoon at me.

I swallowed hard, not at all sure I wanted to eat in this room, where the air smelled of medicine and seemed to press in around me. I saw her fingers jerk open and jumped to catch the spoon as it fell.

"See, things have a habit lately of giving out on me without a moment's notice. Arms, legs, you name it. Anyway, eat up. Whatever I am, I'm not contagious. Besides, the spoon's clean—the soup was inedible and the mystery meat required a hammer and chisel, neither of which I had."

I ate the custard and licked the spoon before I said, "It was good—you should've—"

"Splendid. Now we have a deal. If she sends any more, just run off into one of her hydrangea bushes and eat it all up. Return the dish as nice as you please and we'll all be happy."

"There was something else that I didn't bring," I said. "Some flowers, only they were dead."

"Let me guess," she said, picking up the Cézanne

book I had brought her and holding it without opening it. "Not from Mr. Bigelow, because his flowers
never die—they wouldn't dare. Besides, he wouldn't
send them."

"You're right. He didn't."

"Mattie-Miller's flowers are plastic; that way when
Lad-a-Dog pees on them she can just hose them down.
Let's see—I've got it. Next door. The butcher's wife.
Appropriate somehow. He's a dreadful redneck, and
she's worse. A nothing. The boy must be a throwback."

"She said to give you her lo—" I stopped short, not
wanting to hear what Miss Tegges would say about
David's mother sending her love. "She said to say hi.
The flowers were shot. I think she picked them last
night and forgot to put them in water." I watched as
she sorted through the things I had brought from
home.

"Didn't you bring my checkbook?" she asked, piling
everything up again.

"You didn't mention a checkbook. I don't know—
wouldn't have known where to find it," I said.

"In the left-hand top desk drawer. I knew you should
have written it down. The wretched woman who locks
and unlocks the TV demands her money up front. As
if we're all going to skip out of here under dark of
night. Not that I like TV," she said, bringing her hand
down flat on the table and causing the lunch dishes to
jump. "But, my God, it's something."

"Yes, well—" I went into the bathroom to wash the

custard cup, determined that I wasn't going to apologize for forgetting something I hadn't been told to remember.

"You can bring it tomorrow," Miss Tegges said. "There's a tablet on the windowsill so you can write it down this time. Left-hand top desk drawer."

A nurse came in to take her blood pressure and I moved out of the way, over to the window. She ought to take mine, I thought as I wrote CHECKBOOK in large angry letters and stuffed the piece of paper in my pocket. I could hear the nurse talking in back of me, and Miss Tegges as she mumbled around the thermometer in her mouth.

"So," she said when the nurse had gone. "That puts the TV out of bounds."

I sat on the straight chair wondering how long before I could leave and what there was to talk about until I *did* leave.

"Tell me about Brian Wilgus."

"Brian?"

"Your uncle, Brian Wilgus," Miss Tegges said, kneading her right hand with her left. "Do you know why he does what he does—the collages and the use of textures, the sense of touch that is so strong."

"Because of Gussie, I guess," I said.

"Who's Gussie?"

"My grandmother."

"Why because of Gussie?"

"Because she—well—"

"Go on. I'm awake."

"Collected things. She used to go up and down the streets taking things out of people's trash cans and putting them in her old red wagon. But it wasn't just the collecting she liked. I mean, to Gussie they were beautiful. She saw something in them, in the feathers and stones and bits of marble. And because of that Brian saw it, too. And me."

"And Julie?" she asked.

"No."

"Where is Gussie now?"

It was like my conversation with David Norton all over again, only pricklier. This time I felt I had to defend Gussie, rather than let her stand on her own two feet.

"Well—"

"She's dead. A few weeks ago."

The door swung open and an aide with a wheelchair came in. "Okay, Miss Tegges, they're waiting for you downstairs. Another test."

"I've been waiting for you," Miss Tegges said, looking up from her sketch pad when I went into her room the next day. "Did you find the checkbook?"

I took it out of my bag and put it on the table in front of her.

"It's too late, anyway," she said. "She's gone. Come and gone. Came and went."

"Who?"

"The TV lady."

"Sorry," I said. "Maybe I could find her someplace. There has to be an office or something."

"No office. I thought of that. A transient TV lady. King of the road, as it were, or of the idiot box. But not to worry. I told her to come back after rounds. No, that's not right. Doctors have rounds. TV ladies have —what?"

"Circuits?"

"Routes. TV ladies have routes. Anyway, somewhere some head nurse will see that she comes back. They want me mesmerized. Lulled. They're finished, anyway."

I looked at the pad that Miss Tegges had put on the table—at the faces all out of proportion, the circles that had lost their shape, and the lines that splotched across the page in a way that I was sure was not the way she meant them to be.

"They're *done*," she said, dropping the pencil into the drawer.

"Who's done? What's done?" I asked, looking up from the pages of sketches and back to her.

"The tests. The scans and scams and graphs and what have you. The results are in."

"Oh, that's good. Now can you go home? Did they say—"

"They didn't say. Anything. Yet. The patient is always the last to know. But they *will* say. And I *will* know. Everything.

"Now, tell me some more about you. There you were—wherever there was—with Gussie. And Julie was here. Why?"

Without thinking about it I moved away from the bed and went to sit in the deep armchair in the corner, sinking back, stretching my legs out in front of me. Taking up the story where I had ended it the day before.

"Because Julie left. When I was a couple of weeks old. She put me in Gussie's red wagon and said she was going to the store and went as far as the Trailways bus station and got on the bus."

Out in the hall the voice on the intercom paged Dr. Waggelstein and I waited until it had stopped.

"And Gussie found me a couple of hours later. Asleep. That's all there was, except—" I sat up straight and looked at Miss Tegges as if I had to make her understand this. "She shouldn't have gone. Should've stayed where she was."

"Should. Should. Should," said Miss Tegges. "Who's to say what someone should and shouldn't do. Can do or can't."

She locked her arms across her chest. "Now I'll tell *you* a story about how sometimes people just do what they have to do. Without any looking back," she said abruptly.

The silence in the room stretched between us. An aide came in with a fresh pitcher of ice water, and from down the hall came the sound of someone's television set. Just when I had decided that she was asleep she started to speak.

"It was all so safe and secure where I grew up in North Carolina. Cocoon-like. Baked custard and Sunday school and Dr. Martin from the Episcopal church coming to call. There were Mama and Papa and my three brothers, Francis and Edwin and John. I was the youngest, the only girl. The trouble was that everybody else's cocoon was my straitjacket. It was as though I were fettered there. Even before I knew what it was I had to do, I knew I had to do something. I remember as a child lying in the grass in the back yard and looking up through the trees and feeling as if I were going to explode."

I found myself leaning into Miss Tegges's story—not because I had ever felt fettered, but rather, just the opposite. Because with Gussie I had always felt incredibly free, but with that same waiting-for-something-to-happen feeling she had just described.

Her voice, as she went on, had a faraway quality, so that I looked quickly overhead, as if for a moment I expected to find a giant elm stirring above me.

"And," she went on, "one day Mama came back from a visit to Aunt Sudie in Richmond and she brought me a paint box and a pad of paper. They were watercolors, in a black metal box with indentations in the lid for the water and a place along the side for the brushes. It wasn't long before every one of those oblongs of paint was used up, leaving empty hollows all in a row, with only the corners showing what color each had been.

"And after that it was as if neither the house nor the street, not even the town, could contain me. Papa sent to Richmond for paints and pencils and drawing paper, for my first oils and palette, for brushes by the dozen. There was a teacher at the high school whose greatest gift to me was that she did me no harm. And she showed me books, naming Rembrandt and Michelangelo and Fra Filippo Lippi as if she were turning pages in the family album."

A volunteer stopped at the door with a cart of juice and brought a cup and put it on the table. Miss Tegges peeled back the plastic, tasted it, then let it sit.

"By the time I got to my last year of high school I knew there was no way I could go to Hollins or Randolph-Macon or any of the places the other girls in town were going. I knew that I had to go to art school—or to no school, and just paint. And I fought my parents as if my life depended on it. And my life *did* depend on it.

"Mama took to her bed with a fine case of the vapors. That left only Papa, and I wheedled and begged and pouted and flirted a bit. And with my brothers' help I persuaded him."

The light outside changed and deepened so that the room was in shadow. And still she went on, sort of like a top that would keep spinning until it couldn't spin anymore.

"I came to Baltimore in 1930, to the Maryland Institute. It was the Depression and yet I was peculiarly untouched. I lived in a young ladies' seminary and went to art school and did life drawings and wrote my mother long, impassioned letters on the magnificence of the human body. Think of the relapse, that must have given her vapors," she said, laughing a curious gentle laugh.

"What *are* vapors?" I asked.

"I haven't the foggiest. Something I never believed in is all that I can tell you. Anyway, there were breadlines and men selling apples and artists working for the WPA for $94 a month. There were checks from home, and a song that asked, 'Brother, can you spare a dime?' "

Miss Tegges's voice cracked and grew thinner. She took the juice and drank some of it, and then sat looking into the cup.

"But I couldn't spare anything for anybody. That was the way it had to be. It all had to go into the work I was doing. Then the four years were up and my whole family came for graduation. The day they left to go home I left to go the other way. To New York. And I never went back, except once, for a day or so. Sometimes there are things a person has to do. Sometimes people get hurt. And there's nothing you can do. Do you understand that?"

"No." I stood up suddenly and went over to the window, watching a storm come up: papers blowing on the street below, people running for doorways. "It's not the same thing at all. What you did. Not the same as leaving your own child."

The cup dropped from her hand and rolled under the bed, leaving a trail of pineapple juice. And she shifted onto her side, facing toward the door, making small huffing noises with her mouth. I wiped the juice up with tissues and threw them in the trash. Then I went back to the window, watching the rain and thinking of the anger that had flared inside me. At Julie for leaving all those years ago. I picked up my bag and opened the door just as Dr. Evans was coming into the room.

"Oh, good, someone's here," he said. "I've been hoping I'd hear from your mother. I have to talk to someone about—" He looked over his shoulder at Miss Tegges. "Will you ask her to give me a call?"

"I'm meeting her downstairs in the cafeteria," I said, checking my watch. "Today was her last day at school—she's the school nurse—and afterward she wants to come up to see Miss Tegges. She hasn't been able to get here before. Is she all right? Miss Tegges, I mean? She was awake, and then she was asleep."

"Mmmm, yes," said Dr. Evans. "If your mother would just have me paged after supper, I'll let her know the test results and what Dr. Reinecke, who I've consulted, thinks."

Harper

"THERE'S NOTHING in your head besides art," Mama used to say. "You'd better make room for something else, missy."

And I did, in a big way. It's there now. Gobbling away. Crowding. Pushing.

Christ.

That Dr. Evans came in and woke me up—my mouth all sour with pineapple juice. The girl gone. And starts in at me about something called an intercranial neoplasm.

"Wait," I said. "Say it right out so I can understand."

"Tumor," he said.

"Tumor. Where? What kind? Cranial means—has to do with the— Oh, my God. Brain tumor."

My fingers were digging into the sides of my head as if I could tear it out. Get it out of there. Do you hear me?

He was taking my hands away, putting them down by my side. There, there. Did he really say that? Papa did, when I fell from the apple tree and broke my leg. And that same summer he sent to Richmond for my first set of oil paints. There, there, Harper.

How long ago was that? Not Papa, but Dr. Evans. How many days ago. I've forgotten.

Brain tumor. Yes, that's it. And he left me with the thing still here. Still growing. Pushing inside of me. Get it out, I called as he started for the door.

"Yes, Miss Tegges. That's just what we plan to do."

Smart ass.

I heard the squawk box in the hall paging him.

Slug comes. And sometimes Julie, her mother.

Suzanne. Does Suzanne? No.

I try to draw and the lines—the shapes—like a child would do.

I write notes. To God. To Richard. I don't know where Richard is. I'm not sure about God, either. I have to confess that I'm afraid. Scared as hell . . . scared of hell. H-e-a-t-h-e-n.

I write notes to Papa, too. And Mama. They're both dead now. I went home for Papa's funeral. The boys were there, with wives and children. Nieces and nephews of mine. But by the time my mother was sick I was in California. So far to come, and besides—

I write notes, try to write notes. And the letters jumble together. Do they? Maybe not. Maybe they look that way. Maybe they're fine letters. Fine notes.

. . .

It's tomorrow. The operation. When they're going to go in.

Today. The night was here. Wasn't here. And the sky outside is streaked with pink.

People come in and out of the room. Dancing around. At the time of my first show in New York—and I was afraid because of the critics and the people who would come. Pretend they're all naked, someone said, and you won't be afraid.

They're in and out of the room now. The critics. No. Doctors and nurses. I pretend they're naked. See them all like Matisse's dancing nudes.

Brain surgery is serious, I say.

There, there, Harper.

Julie

"DAMN DOCTORS. Goddamn doctors like that Chickenshit Reinecke. It's people like him that made me get out of hospital nursing this year and take a shot at school nursing."

"Did he really mean what he said?" asked Slug, and for a minute I was surprised to see her there, had thought I was talking to myself. It takes time getting used to a daughter.

"Oh, he meant it all right." Slug and I were sitting in the hospital waiting room surrounded by overflowing ashtrays and old magazines. Harper's surgeon had just left. In fact, he'd left so fast he even managed to stir some of the stale air that settled in around us.

"It's not even so much what he said—I'd pretty much expected that," I said. "It's more the way he came barreling in here to unload his bad news and then go on to the next patient, who may be able to play the game: get well, go home, and bring brownies to the doctor twice a year. More the way he spit out his answers before we barely had time to ask the questions. 'I'm afraid Miss Tegges's tumor is malignant.' 'We did what we could, but now it's a matter of time.' 'The hospital social worker will help make arrangements for a nursing home, since I understand there is no family.' 'She'll need custodial care.' "

I couldn't sit still any longer and had to get up and move around the room. "And then—and then when I asked him how soon he was going to tell her, did you hear what he said?"

"That she didn't need to know," said Slug. "Just to say the operation was a success. That somebody else could see to her affairs."

I swung around to face her, glaring at her as if she were the doctor; saying to her the things I never got a chance to say to him. "Affairs be damned. There are affairs that only she can put in order. Affairs of her heart and her mind and her soul. How *dare* he be the one to decide if Harper Tegges knows whether she is going to live or die." It was as if a thousand firecrackers were going off in my head. I came back and sat on the couch next to Slug. "Besides, Harper made me promise that she would be told the truth."

"But he's the doctor," said Slug, as if everything he said were written in stone.

"Doctors, hah. They set themselves up as little gods —or maybe we set them up that way—and when they come up against something that's bigger than they are, like the thing in Harper Tegges's head, they want to turn and run.

"Oh, what the hell. I guess Dr. Chickenshit Reinecke doesn't want to confront death any more than the rest of us do. Come on. Let's go check if we can see Harper yet."

We pushed through the double doors to the waiting room of the Intensive Care Unit and were immediately confronted by a woman at the desk who was obviously a clone of the one from Admitting.

"Two visitors per patient, immediate family only," she said.

Slug and I pushed on to the next set of doors.

"You are im-med-i-ate family, aren't you?"

"Yes," we both said together as the doors swung shut behind us.

"It's almost an anticlimax, finding her asleep like this." I stood by the side of Harper's bed, holding on to the railing. "I do that a lot—get myself all fired up and then—" I reached out to touch Harper's hand.

"What will the doctor do now?" asked Slug.

"Just what he said. Nothing." I put my finger up to my lips and looked at Slug, mouthing the word "Outside" without saying anything. "Come on. She's sleeping well, which is what she needs. There'll be some fierce kind of pain when she wakes up." For a minute I let my hand hover just above Harper's bandaged head before I drew it back and turned toward the door. "I'll ask them to tell her we were here when she wakes."

. . .

I almost didn't go back to the hospital the next day. But the more I tried not to go, the more I thought about Harper, who had to have one bitch of a headache by now, and Dr. Reinecke leaning over the side of the bed and mouthing platitudes at her. Anyway, when we got there she was awake and staring at the clock.

"They said you had a good night," I said.

Harper made a face, wincing at the effort. "I think that means I didn't make any trouble, though I considered it."

"How about the pain?"

"Bad."

"Slug's here with me," I said, stepping back.

And Harper raised her right hand inches off the bed and let it drop again. She tried to move her head, then stopped, clutching the top sheet in her hand.

"The tumor—the thing in my head—it was malignant, wasn't it?" she said.

"What did Dr. Reinecke tell you?" I asked, playing for time.

"Dr.— Who's—"

"The neurosurgeon. The one who operated on you," I said.

"Oh, him." Harper unclenched her fingers, but the wad of sheet stayed crumpled there.

The clock on the wall rasped and jerked forward.

"It's what he *didn't* say," Harper said. "But it was, wasn't it?"

Through the glass partition I looked out at the nurses' station, at the monitors and machines and dials and buttons.

"It *was*, wasn't it?" said Harper again, her fingers opening and closing on the bed beside her.

"Yes. Yes, it is," I said, slipping my finger into her claw-like grasp. "But there's always the chance that something—that someone—" I just couldn't knock all the props out from under her.

I wanted to turn away from Harper's face and the emotions that played themselves out across it, made all the more grotesque by the swath of bandage that bound her head and dipped onto her forehead. But Harper still had hold of my finger, pulling me forward so that I had to plant my legs against the bed to keep from losing my balance.

"Well, that's good," said Harper, her voice suddenly strong. "They found it—and operated. Now I can get on with my life—work to be—"

I heard Slug gasp, and from somewhere far away I saw her move toward the door. "I'm going to the library. I need something to read and Henley wrote me about this book—I want to see if it's in. Don't wait. I'll take the bus home."

Harper let go of my finger, but it was a long time before I was able to pull it away, watching, instead, as it went from white to angry red to white again.

"Now that that's over," said Harper as I straightened up, resting my hands on the side of the bed, cooling my finger on the metal, "I want to get in touch with my gallery, the people who take care of my affairs, as soon as I get into a room with a telephone. There was talk of a retrospective. I have to let them know."

I saw the glassy look in Harper's eyes and the way her fingers still worried the sheet as she said fretfully, "There are people I have to call. There are—"

NO, something screamed inside my head. You're not listening to me. I said *is* and not *was*. The tumor in your head *is* malignant. It's cancer and they're talking about custodial care and you're talking about a show, for god's sake.

"I need more paper and pencils, because I have notes to write." Harper's face was streaked with exhaustion, but she went on. "And once I'm home . . ."

A nurse appeared in the doorway, speaking first to me as she said, "The ten minutes are up. Tomorrow they'll be moving her to a regular room and you can visit longer."

And then to Harper, "Now, let's not tire ourselves, Miss Tegges."

I touched Harper on the hand and turned to go.

"Pissants," I heard her say. "There's damn little 'ourselves' about it. If *you're* tired, take a nap."

But I saw, as I looked over my shoulder, that Harper's eyes were closed, her head dropping to one side, her mouth open.

.   .   .

"I'm not going to see Harper today," said Slug the next day after lunch. "I can't go. I can't stand it." She waited as if expecting me to argue with her, and when I didn't she went on: "It's grotesque. It's gross. I mean, she didn't even *hear* you."

"I think she heard me," I said.

"How could she—and go on talking about her life and her work?"

"How could she and *not* go on talking about them?" I said, feeling that I had to make her understand.

"I don't get it." Slug took her lunch dishes to the sink and started to wash them.

"What I think is that Harper knows what is going to happen to her, but she's not ready to know it yet. So she has to go on talking about her plans, denying what's happening inside her head. Until she's able to—"

"It's a waste of time," said Slug, turning the water up as hard as it would go and standing with her back to me. "Why doesn't she just—"

"What?" I said, raising my voice above the sound of running water. "Just give in, curl up and suck her thumb? Is that what you expect?" I wanted to pull Slug away from the sink, turn her around, and tell her to stop being so young and so damn absolute. Then I realized that she *was* young—and with the young, things *are* absolute. And what was I doing with this stranger in my house, anyway? Me the mother. Hah.

Okay, Julie, I thought, let's try again. Take it from the top. "There was a poem I heard once that I've never forgotten. It was by Dylan Thomas and it went, 'Do not go gentle into that good night . . .' Let Harper Tegges have her chance to curse and bless. The rest will come."

"Well, I still don't know whether I want to visit her," said Slug.

"That's up to you."

"Now that I know she's going to die. I mean, with Gussie things were different. It just happened. But this—with Miss Tegges—to know it and watch it happen—"

"I understand how you feel," I said, suddenly sympathetic.

"What's this whole thing with Miss Tegges to you, anyway?" Slug turned around, wiping her hands on her shorts.

There went the sympathy shot to hell. "I don't know what it is to me except that, like it or not, I seem to be involved." I scraped my plate into the trash, rubbing at mayonnaise and bits of potato chips harder than was warranted.

"No. The truth bit, I mean," said Slug. "Why not let her believe that everything's all right? Like Dr. Reinecke said."

"Dr. Chickenshit."

"Why not?"

"Because I don't think most people want to live like

that. To die like that. Everyone has affairs of one kind or another to put in order. For crying out loud, this is something pretty big we're talking about. And the truth is too important to put on hold at a time like this."

"Truth—truth— Fat lot you know about truth," said Slug. "There are things I've wanted to know. Truth I've wanted to be told."

"Why did I leave, all those years ago? Is that it?" I went to stand by the back door, bracing myself for the question I'd known, sooner or later, was going to come.

"Oh no. Not that. Not yet, anyway. What I want to know is who my father is."

For a minute it was as if the wind had been knocked out of me and I had to concentrate on getting it back, on just breathing in and out. It seemed hours before I was able to speak.

"I don't know," I said, still facing out the door.

"I don't know.

"My God, I don't know."

I stood by the side of Harper's bed in her room on the ninth floor later that afternoon, fielding questions like a politician at a press conference. "Hey, wait. I'll take these in order. First the dog. The dog is fine. Slug's been walking her a lot, and Mattie-Miller sent dog Yummies in a basket with a yellow ribbon."

"Vomit," said Harper, flat on her back and looking up at the ceiling.

"Next, I don't *know* how long before you get out of here.

"And Slug's—Slug is back at the library again. When she got there yesterday she, uh, she didn't have Henley's letter with the name of the book she was supposed to get. So she had to go back."

Harper fumbled with the buttons on the side of the bed, and soon the top half of the mattress began to rise. "There," she said, pointing to the tray table. "Notes I wrote about things to do, people to call. Read them." She pushed papers toward me.

I took the pages, shuffling them without looking at them.

"Read them," Harper insisted.

"Westall Gallery," I read, and then a hodgepodge of numbers that seemed to be piled one on top of another. I turned the paper over.

> *Bedpans are the devil's invention—*
> *If Richard comes*
> *The operation was very succes—*
> *I never really knew what pain was—*
> *It's been hell but now a painting—*

The words were crouched to the side of the page, so that I found myself looking around for the rest of them, thinking, for a minute, of the ends of Harper's thoughts free-floating around the room.

I took up another page and saw names repeated there: *Richard—Suzanne—Slug—Richard—Suzanne—*

"I tried to make a long-distance call but they wouldn't let me," said Harper, tugging at the edge of her bandage. "So if you would, from my phone at home, call the gallery for me. Tell them to send someone down here. Tell them there's work to be done."

"Well, yes, I guess I could." I heard myself waffling and wished for a nurse to come with a bedpan or a thermometer or something.

"The number's there somewhere," said Harper, moving her fingers as if she herself were rattling papers.

I rooted through the pages for the one covered over with numbers and stood staring down at it, trying to disentangle one from another. I finally had to say, "I can't make the numbers out."

And Harper held her hand out for the piece of paper, pulling it close, then pushing it away. She turned it sideways and upside down before she let it fall to the floor. "The pen wasn't good," she said. "I'll tell it to you and *you* write it down."

Digging paper and a pen out of my bag, I sat waiting.

"It's—it's—" Harper looked around the room. She rubbed at a place just between her eyes and curled an edge of bandage. "Two—two—uh— It's— Wait. I know—always knew it before. Called there, or they called me. And now someone's playing tricks. Things that were there are gone. I don't know it anymore," she said in a voice that seemed to be winding down. She pushed the button at the side of the bed again, and when the mattress was flat she lay with her hands clenched by her sides.

"Don't worry about it," I said as I looked away from the questioning in her face. "It will come to you. Or I can ask Information. Listen, I'm terrible with numbers myself. Everybody is." Shut up, Julie, I thought. You're pushing it. And I forced myself to turn back to her.

"It's nice out," I said to Harper, who was staring up at the ceiling and looked oddly like a mummy lying there. "Not too hot and—" I thought about what difference the weather would make to someone who wasn't going anyplace and cast about for something else to say. "About Slug—" I said, trying to think what I was going to say about Slug. "Sometimes when she's walking Ginger she stops to talk to that David Norton, who lives next door to you. Do you know him?"

"No. Yes. Not really," said Harper, without turning her head. "He's helped me with things in the house and in the yard. I know that he cares about the work he does."

"The car?"

"No. That's what he does so he can do what he wants to do. He hasn't said much, and I haven't asked because I can't—I never could—never wanted to know any of them very well. What about him?"

"Oh, nothing, except that I'm glad Slug has someone to talk to. Maybe when school starts she'll find more friends. She needs someone she can trust."

Harper waved vaguely in the direction of the glass of water on the table beside her.

I held the glass with its bent straw and let her drink, watching as she swiped at a trickle of water running off her chin and onto the pillow. "She trusted Gussie, didn't she?" Harper said.

"Slug? Yes, she trusted Gussie. But not me. Never me." I sat down on the straight chair by the side of the bed, not sure whether I was talking to myself or to Harper, who seemed to have drifted into a doze.

"I left her just after she was born," I said.

"Yes," said Harper.

"She told you, then?"

"Yes."

"She asked me today—I can't believe it was only today—she asked me who her father was. And I had to tell her I didn't know."

I kneaded the back of my neck with my fingers, pressing the skin until it hurt. "Of course, I didn't have to tell her that. I could have picked one, anyone. Take a card. Take any card. Billy Wilkins or Warren Fitz-Hugh. Bobby Dickinson. Tom, Dick, or Harry. Any high-school boy with a hard-on. I was like a dog in heat. I flaunted it. Gave it away. And they took it. In the backs of cars and pickup trucks—and once in a hay wagon when everybody else was eating watermelon on the beach. Between sex and watermelon I'd've rather had the watermelon. But I was what they called loose. An easy lay. And I was pregnant by the time I was seventeen."

I moved away from the bed, going to sit on the windowsill, wanting to stop the flow of words. But when Harper's "And—" prompted me, I heard myself going on.

"I had my baby and I named her Mary Rose October, and I tried to like her. But one day I was overcome by this terrific urge to leave, so that it was all I could do to wait for the next bus to anywhere.

"It's funny, but all the things I had to get away from were the things that Slug has told me she loved best. The poky little house. My mother, Gussie, who wasn't like anybody else's mother in the whole town, and her ESP, or whatever it was, and people coming to the house and bribing her to tell them things. 'Here's a bundle for you, Gussie. Some clothes, used but serviceable. For your children. For you. And books— some of the pages are torn but—' Good enough for the likes of you is what they meant. They traded their pasts for shiny new futures, and Gussie let them do it.

"And my father, who was struck by lightning and killed, his shoe split clear through. She kept it in a brown paper bag under the daybed. And there was Brian, who was better and brighter and sure, we always knew, to do something wonderful.

"And the things Slug wouldn't know about. The baby who cried and cried. The Slug-baby. The way people on the street looked at me. The mothers and fathers of the Billys, Warrens, the Bobbys. And somewhere among those lookers were the grandparents of my baby.

"And the way Gussie didn't look at me."

I stopped, waiting until the sound of my voice had seeped out of the room. Then I went on: "And Gussie's fascination with junk and the clutter she brought home. Picking out of people's trash cans, and the time she got the red wagon, nearly new, from Fitchett Brothers' Secondhand. One day I grabbed that baby and said the first thing that came into my mind, that I needed diaper pins. Diaper pins, for god's sake. I put her in Gussie's wagon and bounced her along down Nectarine Street to Main. The way Gussie went looking for treasure. And I left the wagon—and the baby —at the bus depot."

Harper moved her fingers as if to say that she was awake, and I went on. I would have gone on, anyway. I couldn't stop.

"Isn't it funny how things are determined by chance? I mean, the first bus was going to New York, so I went to New York. I sometimes wonder what might have happened if that bus had been going to Philadelphia or Atlantic City. Or even Norfolk.

"But I went to New York, when I had never been

out of that little town on the eastern shore of Virginia. When I'd never learned anything from a mother who was too busy seeing what others couldn't see.

"It was 1967, and I was an accident waiting to happen. I was rejecting an establishment I didn't even know existed. I was part of an 'alternative society' when life with Gussie was more 'alternative society' than I could handle."

I looked across the room and saw Slug standing just inside the door. I didn't know how long she had been there but I could tell from her face that she had heard every word I said. The odd thing was that I was *glad* she'd heard. Glad that she knew. We looked at each other—a long, hard look—and before I could move, Slug turned and went out of the room. And I let her go.

I got up slowly, feeling numb and cramped, and went to stand beside Harper's bed. "I'm sorry," I said, "for going on like that. I don't know why I did—don't usually. But when Slug asked me that question today—"

"No. It was all right," Harper said. Her eyes seemed to skew around the room before she said, "I've been thinking about the show. There are several paintings at home, finished, or almost so. They didn't get it all, did they? The cancer, I mean."

For a minute I waited to see if Harper would go on to something else, but she was looking up at me, her expression, below the bandage, almost rakish.

"They didn't, did they?" she said again.

I wasn't sure what I was going to say, but was determined to let Harper talk if she wanted to. I reached for her hand, but she pulled back, closing her eyes and saying, "Not now."

The next time I went to see Harper, she was sitting propped up in bed. Her bandage was gone and her head, shaved for the operation, had a hook-shaped scar dipping down one side. "Get me out of here," she shouted. "Get me out of here."

I stood in the doorway as if I were caught in a storm, while Harper's words drummed around me. I almost wished I was back at the dentist's—anywhere but here.

The floor nurse came up behind me, edging me into the room, so that together we moved into the torrent of Harper's words.

"Goddamn it, where have you been?" said Harper, shaking her fist at me, then watching as her arm jerked sideways, faltered, and dropped to the bed. "It's been forever since you—"

"Day before yesterday," I said, wondering what had gone on in Harper's life since then. "It seems like a long time to you, doesn't it?"

"Damn right it does." Harper pressed her head back against the pillow and closed her eyes, stroking her right hand rhythmically with her left. "Has Richard come? Called? Mama and Papa and the boys?" Her eyes opened wide as if she was suddenly aware of what she had said. She went on quickly: "I don't like it here. The food is rank, and the noise—"

The nurse moved to the bed, holding a paper cup of pills in one hand, pouring water into a glass with the other. "Now, Miss Tegges," she said.

"No," said Harper as she reared up, swatting the cup so that it flew across the room, the pills making small clicking noises as they fell to the floor.

I ran forward, pulling a chair away from the wall, helping the nurse look for the pills, anything rather than having to confront Harper's anger.

"That's the lot," the nurse said, straightening up and holding a hand out to me. "I'll get new ones and bring them back." And she was gone, leaving me alone in the room with Harper. I tried to think of something to say.

Harper reached out and took the glass of water off the bedside table and lifted it slowly, opening and closing her mouth as she tried to catch the straw. I started to move forward to help her, caught myself, and stayed where I was. I watched the water level of the glass drop as Harper clamped the straw between her lips and sucked, then saw it bubble up as she let it go without swallowing. After a minute Harper took the glass away from her mouth and swung it in the direction of the table. Her fingers flew open and the glass fell, bouncing off the partly open drawer and crashing down onto the floor.

"I'll get it," I said, glad to have something to do.

"Why?" said Harper.

"To get the water cleaned up—the glass."

"Why?" said Harper again, and something in the tone of her voice made me stop and move closer to the bed, stepping in the puddle of spilled water, the shards of broken glass.

"Why me?" said Harper. "Why me? Why me? Why me?" Her voice got progressively louder. "Goddamn it to hell, why me?"

"I don't know," I said.

"Why now?" said Harper, rubbing her hand over the back of her head. "Now I have things to do. Now I have—like the Fourth of July."

"It's only June," I said, knowing even as I said it that Harper and I were operating on different wavelengths.

"And the picnic up the road at Aunt Annie and Uncle Millard's place." I tried to follow along with her.

"Measles," said Harper. "And a sore throat and pains in my head." She reached up to her head again, first with one hand and then the other, a look of confusion passing across her face. "And the day before the picnic—the day before the Fourth of July—the spots started to come out."

"You got the measles for the Fourth of July?" I said, pulling a chair up, hearing it grate against the broken glass.

For a moment Harper glared at me as if I had intruded on something. She looked beyond me and went on: "I was in bed with the shades pulled down, the dark-green summer shades, mind you, and food brought up on a tray, and sponge baths and alcohol rubs—" She shivered as if the cold alcohol was again splashing over her body. "And no visitors except Mama, and Papa from the doorway.

"Mama stayed home from the picnic on the Fourth of July, sitting in the corner of the screened porch and coming up from time to time with cool cloths and cups of crushed ice. I could hear her crushing it on the kitchen table, the sound carrying up the back steps. I knew she was there with the chunks of ice wrapped in a kitchen towel, whacking away with a wooden mallet with ridges dug into it."

Harper clenched her fists and brought them down hard, one after another, on the tops of her thighs.

"Stop," I said, reaching out, but not quite touching her pounding hands. "You'll hurt—"

"I hurt," said Harper, stopping her fists in midthrust as if she needed her strength to go on. "Oh, Christ, I hurt.

"And the day after the Fourth of July," she went on, "John came sneaking into the room with E. Nesbit's dragon stories. He pulled the painted rocker over to the window, holding the shade out an inch or two and the book up to the light, and he read them to me. And when they were done he read them over again. Running like a jackrabbit when he heard Mama coming, until she found him out and said he was already exposed and if he was going to get measles he was going to get them.

"And when he did I sat on the rocker in John's room and pulled the shade out a mite and read the dragon stories yet another time." There was a long silence; then Harper said, "I still remember some of it. 'He happened to be building a palace when the news came, and he left all the blocks kicking about the floor for nurse to clear up—but then the news was rather remarkable news . . .' "

I blinked my eyes as if surprised not to find myself in Harper's darkened room. Or John's. "John was—"

"My brother, the one closest to my age. We were almost like twins; Irish twins, they used to say. Only we weren't Irish.

" 'Remarkable news,' " said Harper, reaching back to the dragon stories.

"Remarkable news," she said even louder. "That there's something in my head and it's— Then it will—"

I got up and pushed the chair to the dry part of the floor. I went into the bathroom and came back with paper towels, mopping at the water, the broken glass; dropping the sodden lumps into the trash can.

"Why does it have to be me? Just tell me that. And what will happen to me? Where will I go? Did Richard call? Good God, I don't know where Richard is. It's been so long—and I want water. I want it now."

I stood up, holding on to the back of the chair, feeling as if I were standing in the ocean, bracing myself against another wave of Harper's anger.

The nurse came back, left, and came again with a clean glass wrapped in plastic. I unwrapped it and held it out while she poured the water. Then, taking a straw out of the drawer, I held the glass toward Harper, guiding the straw into her mouth, watching while she swallowed the pills one after another.

Without saying anything else Harper pushed the button to lower her bed and lay still, her anger spent.

After a few minutes I turned and went out of the room. As I headed for the elevator I stopped at the nurses' station, leaning on the counter and staring at a bowl of pansies, running my finger along their velvety faces. When the nurse put down the telephone I said, "How long has Miss Tegges been the way she is now?"

"This angry? Last couple of days. It's rough, isn't it? Not that I blame her. I'd probably be worse—tear the place apart at the seams."

"Yes, it's rough," I said.

"Especially not having any family. Apparently all her brothers are dead."

"She talks about a Richard, but I don't know who he is."

A doctor waited with a chart and the nurse turned away. The elevator came and I ran for it, stepping to the back and leaning against the wall, feeling completely drained.

. . .

"I went to the hospital to see Miss Tegges," said Slug, coming into the house later that afternoon. "I waited here but you didn't come back from the dentist, so I figured you had changed your mind. That you had something else you wanted to do."

Right on, kid, I thought. An orgy. An orgy in the afternoon at the no-tell motel. Just me and—and— who the hell *would* it be— There was something in her tone that sounded as if she was accusing me, as if she was attacking me for the things she heard in Harper's room that day. "I got tied up," I said. "But I was here. I said I would be, and I was." And don't keep punishing me, I wanted to say as I met Slug's eyes and held them until she finally looked away.

"It doesn't matter," said Slug, dropping her things on the table with a thud that said it certainly did. "I went to the library and then up to see Miss Tegges. She was pretty wild."

"Yes," I said. "I was there earlier."

"She threw the pudding off her tray at the dietitian when she came to ask about the meals. And she called Dr. Reinecke a 'fat fucking pig.' Her words, not mine," she said quickly.

I started to laugh, then choked it back, knowing somehow that a proper mother wouldn't do that, even though they were my sentiments exactly.

"One of the aides brought her a ruffly cap—a boudoir cap, she called it—to wear now that her bandages are gone. And Miss Tegges ripped it apart and threw it on the floor.

"After that the nursing supervisor came around and said she would like to talk to Miss Tegges, please, and closed the door with me on the other side. And all the way down the hall to the elevator I could hear her—Miss Tegges, I mean. If you think what she called Dr. Reinecke was bad you should've heard—"

"She's angry," I said.

"No kidding," said Slug.

"Wouldn't you be? I would. She's got a lot to be angry about. In fact, right now anger's eating into her faster than the cancer."

"Will it stop?"

"The anger will, I hope. As for the cancer, it's too far gone. You know that. I guess all we can hope for Harper is that she comes to some kind of acceptance."

After a minute Slug grabbed her books off the table, dropping one, picking it up, and dropping another. She slung the strap of her pocketbook over her shoulder as she headed out the door.

I stood by the table and listened to her clatter up the steps; heard doors slamming overhead, the whine of bedsprings. It's too much, I thought. Trying to talk to her about mortality when we can hardly talk about the weather. I should've come straight home from the dentist, taken her to the museum or someplace.

The noises upstairs seemed to go into reverse. The bedsprings yowled; feet slapped overhead; there was the sound of running water, a racketing on the stairway.

"I'm trying to understand," said Slug from the kitchen door, rubbing at the water on her face and the edges of her hair, tossing the towel onto the chair. "This whole business of acceptance. I'm working on it." She went to the refrigerator, pulling out lettuce and tomatoes and carrots, rummaging under the sink for an onion. "I'll make the salad," she said. Then whacking the lettuce on the drainboard to loosen the stem, she swung around to face me. "But what's the point? She can't win anyway."

"It's not a contest. I guess it has to do with the quality of the time Harper has left."

"So what will happen to her? Where will they send her? What will it be like?"

"That's what I've been thinking about," I said, opening a can of tuna fish and dumping it into a bowl. "I've been trying to figure it out."

"And?"

"If only Harper had someone to look after her, she could go home. And maybe we should do it."

"Who?"

"Us. All of us. You and me. Ernestus Stokes. Mattie-Miller. The Nortons, and maybe Mr. Bigelow."

"Do what?"

"Help to take care of her. So that Harper Tegges can come home to die."

"Why us?"

"There isn't anyone else."

"But why bring her home at all? I mean, what's wrong with the hospital?"

"Because Harper has been asking to come home. And because people shouldn't die alone. There should be somebody to hold their hand, or do whatever. And hospitals are—did you ever hear the old joke about marriage being a wonderful institution but who wants to live in an institution? Well, who wants to die in one?" I added onions and mayonnaise to the tuna fish and turned it onto a plate before I went on.

"And because, I guess when it comes right down to it, it's something I *want* to do. I was never really there to take care of anyone. Not you—"

"You could have been," said Slug.

"Or my father. Or Gussie. Not even Monica."

"Who's Monica?"

Maybe that's what this is all about, I thought. Even more than my mother and my father—that when Monica died I wasn't there. That I turned and ran away.

"Who's Monica?" said Slug again.

"She's—she was my friend."

"What happened to her?" Slug leaned across the table as if she could push me to go on.

"I came out of the bus station that day," I began.

"The day you left me in Gussie's wagon?"

"I came out of the bus station and into the world. And what a world it was. Remember, for me excitement had been watching the farmers come into town on Saturday afternoons or a dance in the school gym.

"And there I was in New York City, surrounded by more noise than I had ever heard in my life. More everything: cars, taxicabs, buses, trucks—all blowing their horns. More dirt. More smells. More excitement. Music pouring out of doorways. Lights blinking around me, but I couldn't see the sky. Garbage cans heaped along the curbs. What would Gussie have done with all of them, I thought. I didn't *care* what Gussie would've done. She was in the past and I was in the present.

"I was pushed along by the crowd and afraid to cross the street and drunk with the excitement of what was going on around me all at the same time.

"But remember, I had just had a baby."

"Me," said Slug.

"You. And I was beginning to hurt. My legs, my back. As if everything inside me was going to gush right out onto the sidewalk.

"It started to rain and I backed into a doorway with a sign taped onto the glass: HELP WANTED. Red letters on black cardboard, curling at the edges. That's what I needed: help. Then I realized that I was the help that somebody else wanted. I pushed my way in against the people coming out. Smell piled on top of smell, fish

and sausage and pickled everything, and none of it like
Daisy's Luncheonette back home."

I got up and poured two glasses of iced tea; I came
back to the table, handing one to Slug.

"There was a man in an apron behind the cash
register. He had black hair on his arms that curled like
fur.

" 'I've come about the job,' I said.

" 'What job?' he said.

" 'The job in the window.'

" 'Doing what?' Fur arms went on.

" 'Anything.' I was past caring that I sounded
desperate.

"He came out from behind the cash register and
looked down at me. Poking at my suitcase. Kicking it,
you might say. 'Jesus H. Christ,' he said. 'Now they
come bag and baggage straight from the farm. Experience?'

" 'Yes,' I said.

" 'I'm sure you have, girlie. Waitressing, I mean.'

" 'Yes.' I didn't want the stupid job anymore—and
I ached with wanting it. I was feeling a little crazy.
And I wanted to throw up.

" 'Good God, Bennie, leave her alone.' A tall girl
with a thousand freckles and red hair pulled back from
her face was between the two of us. 'You got a job, she
needs a job. Why don't the two of you get it together.'

"A man came up behind me, waiting to get to the

cash register, and stood picking his teeth with his check.

" 'Give her a chance,' the redhead said.

" 'Okay, girlie. Bring all your tips to me and I'll give you what I think you're worth.'

" 'Bullshit, Bennie. A job's a job. She gets the same as the rest of us.' The redhead grabbed my suitcase and pushed me between the tables to the back of the restaurant. 'Don't let him hustle you, okay. You are looking kind of peaky, though. You all right?'

" 'Yes,' I said. 'And thanks.' "

"And that was Monica?" said Slug, pushing her chair back on two legs and reaching for a bag of cookies.

"That was Monica," I said. "Hey, it's time for that dog to go out. Do you want to or shall I?"

Slug got up slowly. "She could go later. I could—"

"No," I said. "Poor thing, over there alone, cooped up. But Harper had such a fit when I told her Mattie-Miller offered to take the dog."

"I'll go," said Slug. "But I'll be right back. You won't—you're still—" ·

"Yes," I said. "I'll wait."

When Slug came back a few minutes later she brought Ginger with her, letting the dog into the kitchen and giving her milk in a bowl with a crack down the side.

I sat where I was, watching the dog finish the milk and lie down on the floor in front of the door. Slug took the plates off the table, scraped them, and put them in the sink, watching me all the while as if I might mysteriously disappear.

"Had you ever been a waitress before?" she asked.

"No," I said. "Our town never was big on restaurants, and I guess that hasn't changed much. Daisy's Luncheonette, and the Dinner Bell. I stocked shelves in Mr. Trimper's dry-goods store one summer, and sometimes Mrs. Trimper had me come around and scrub the spindles on her porch with a toothbrush. I hated that town."

"I liked it," said Slug, looking straight at me. And I thought for a minute that the conversation might end right there.

"Anyway, when it was time for the deli to close—Jake's Deli, only there wasn't any Jake, just Bennie—Monica asked me if I had a place to stay, and before I could make up my mind whether to lie or not, she picked up my suitcase and was pushing me out the door. And I had my first subway ride. Aboveground was one thing, but underground I saw—well, compared to what I was used to on Main Street, it was like a walking freak show.

"We went back to an apartment that was somebody's. Everybody's. There were people sitting and talking, and they moved over to make a place for me.

But I saw a broken-down old chair and crawled into it like a cat; in fact, I think I had to throw a cat out of the way to make room for me. The talk went on all night and the air was thick with the smell of pot. Somebody had a guitar. Somebody sang.

"In the morning I couldn't find Monica right away. I found a bathroom, though, and my suitcase, and something clean to wear. But my clothes didn't look like anybody else's clothes—they never had and they didn't then. Someone gave me a cup of coffee, asked me my name and what I thought of the war. What war? I knew about the war but I didn't know. Someone sang 'Ode to Billy Joe,' and I knew that whoever she was she had sung it through the night. I had heard the words over and over, all about Billy Joe McAllister jumping off the Tallahatchie Bridge.

"Monica and I went to work that day. And the days after that, for a while at least. But when there was a little money or when we didn't care, we didn't go. Sometimes we took to the streets, panhandling.

"I let my hair grow, got rid of the clothes from Trimper's Dry Goods, and I looked like everybody else. The way I wanted to look. For the first time in my life I had this overwhelming feeling of belonging.

"We moved a lot, but the apartments all looked the same. We slid from one year to the next, and it was as if the world were going crazy. Martin Luther King was assassinated, and I wanted to call Gussie and ask her if she knew who he was and if she cared. When Bobby Kennedy was killed, I got as far as the phone booth. I wanted to wake Gussie up, wake that whole stifled town up and ask them if they knew what was going on.

"But for me life was what kept going on. And we were *doing* things, only now, looking back, it seems as if the *idea* of doing was more important than what we did.

"And we talked. Boy, did we talk. Sometimes it was like having a part in a long-running play. I mean, the cast of characters kept changing, but the action stayed the same. Except Monica, she was always there. But in a way even *she* had changed.

"We were all a part of what was going on. We weren't students, but we marched with them. Protested with them."

"Protested what?" said Slug.

"Anything. Everything. Except love. We were all for love."

"We went to Woodstock and listened to Joan Baez singing 'Drug Store Truck Drivin' Man' and 'Joe Hill.' It rained and we wallowed in the mud and thought it was terrific. The funny thing is that now, if I get my feet wet, I can't wait to change my shoes. But it was different then. I lost my shoes, my backpack, most of my clothes. For a while I thought I had lost Monica and Bob and Sam and whoever, but we all got together again and went back to the city."

I stopped for a minute and then went on: "It wasn't long after that that I lost Monica for good—and that has to have been the worst time of my life."

Slug gasped, and when I looked up, it was as if she had pulled away from me. The table seemed to stretch for miles between us, and I read on her face what she had just heard me say: that losing Monica was harder than losing Slug.

For a minute I wanted to reach out to her, to take it back—but I started talking again, all the hurt of that one night in New York tearing at me from inside.

"I had been out somewhere, and when I came in I found her on the floor. I'd never seen her like this before, even though I knew she'd been doing heroin. I'd begged her to stop. To—" I closed my eyes and saw it all: the way her red hair looked against the wide worn floorboards of the apartment and that funny, tattery, rag rug bunched under the couch. Suddenly I was in that room again and it was too much.

I opened my eyes, staring at the kitchen window and the remains of daylight. "I got an ambulance and went with her to the hospital, but then they started asking questions. Names. How long had she been doing this? Dates. They said that maybe Monica wasn't going to make it and for me to have a seat in the waiting room. I heard them talking—the doctors, and then the police. Talking, and looking over at me, at where I'd had a seat like they told me to do. I was scared. For Monica, and for me. That somehow they would find out

Gussie's name and send me home. Back to there. And I ran. I called her parents long distance from a phone booth and promised to meet them when they got to the city. And I ran again.

"I called the hospital from around the corner and they wouldn't tell me anything. After a while I went creeping into the Emergency Room like an animal, and the girl at the desk told me that Monica had died. I wanted to go to her: to see her and touch her and hold her. A doctor started toward me, and a nurse. 'Wait,' they said. 'We want to talk to you.' The police were there, too—pigs we called them then. And I was sure that Gussie had sent them. To make me go back so I could take care of— I mean, Monica was gone and I had to get away, too. I turned and ran again, and kept on running until I couldn't run anymore."

"Were you—you and Monica—" Slug started, then stopped, looking at me through the shadows.

"I loved her. But we weren't lovers. She was my friend."

"But you left her there—even before she died." Slug said the words flatly, with no question in her voice, but when I looked at her she was crying.

"I left her. And—don't say it—before that I left you."

"And never wanted to come back," said Slug.

"No. I never wanted to go back. I *couldn't* go back." The kitchen was almost dark. From the next street over came the sound of children calling, "Oley oley in free."

Somewhere a dog barked. Slug got up and reached for the light switch, then changing her mind, she went out onto the back porch and came in carrying a candle in a red glass container crisscrossed with net. She struck a match and the wick flared up for a minute, before settling into a steady glow. The smell of citronella filled the room.

"That was it. I went back to the apartment, got whatever money there was, a few clothes, and found a room alone. After that I spent a rock-bottom time trying to come to terms with myself. And I stayed alone from then on."

"Until I came," said Slug.

"Yes. I got a job in another deli and spent only what I had to spend, and finally started to get my life in some kind of order. After a while I had enough to put myself through one year of nursing school. I'm not exactly sure how or why I knew that was what I had to do, but it had something to do with the way I felt when I got Monica to the hospital that night. Even with what happened. A feeling that somebody was there, in spite of all the screwed-up things we'd done.

"One night I found a Baltimore paper on the subway and I picked it up to do the crossword puzzle—only it was already done. I was telling Harper the other day how my life has always been decided by chance—where the bus was going or what city the paper was from. So I came to Baltimore and got a room on Maryland Avenue and found a nursing school. Somehow I knew that a run-of-the-mill application by mail wasn't going to get me anywhere, so I practically camped on their doorstep. I threw myself at them, made myself a real pain in the ass, so that finally they gave me an interview. That was all I wanted. Afterward there were high-school equivalency tests, more interviews, the whole shmeer. And I got in. 'How can you pay?' the director of admissions asked. She was a tough old bird. 'I have enough for one year,' I said. 'And then I'll need a scholarship.' She laughed and slapped her desk and said, 'Go to it, Julie Wilgus. Go to it.' "

"And you did," said Slug, blowing out the candle and standing up, this time turning on the light.

"Yes, I did," I said. "And maybe because of all that I don't want Harper Tegges to die alone."

Slug stood blinking at the clutter of dirty dishes and the carrot peelings, which had dried and formed a pattern in the sink. "It's just that, for me at least, things keep getting in the way," she said.

More than anything, I wanted to be by myself. "We'll talk about it another time. Tomorrow, or— You go do something with this dog and I'll clean up here."

The next morning I was alone in the kitchen when Ernestus Stokes arrived.

"Now, Miss Wilgus," she said as soon as I opened

the door, "if you have a few minutes I'd like to talk to you about Harper Tegges."

"Could I get you a cup of coffee?" I asked as I showed her into the living room. "I was just—"

"No, indeed. I had my breakfast hours ago," she said in a voice that clearly implied that the better part of the day was already behind her. "I went to the hospital last night to see Harper Tegges. We were never friends, mind you, but being neighbors one does one's duty. They're talking about a nursing home. A social worker was just leaving as I got to the room, and I heard her say it right out loud. Nursing home. And Miss Tegges was upset, make no mistake about that. The water pitcher went over. I wouldn't want to say how. And a glass. Things out of the drawer. She couldn't know it's cancer, the way she was talking about an exhibit she's planning to have in New York somewhere."

"She knows. Some of the time, at least," I said, watching Slug, wrapped in a yellow terry-cloth robe, sit her way down the steps and stop just before she got to the bottom. She peered through the spindles across the hall and into the living room.

"There ought to be some other way," Ernestus Stokes's voice pushed on. "Both my mother and father were cared for at home."

"There is no family."

"More's the pity."

"Well yes, but— Slug and I were talking about Harper's situation just last night," I said. Before I laid my whole life out there, like so many fish tossed onto a dock, I thought.

"I don't know the state of her finances—I'm not familiar with any artists. Nursing care can be prohibitive. Not to mention finding the right ones. Round the clock, I should think. But as a neighbor, a Christian neighbor, I'd be glad to do my part. And so would Mattie-Miller. I spoke to her earlier this morning."

"It's good of you to be concerned," I said, moving into the hall and watching out of the corner of my eye as Slug scooted back up the stairs. I held open the front door and waited for Ernestus Stokes to leave, following her onto the porch and saying, "If I think of any way we can help—" I couldn't explain to her that it was up to Slug: that I couldn't get into this unless she was willing.

"You'll be in touch?" Miss Stokes said as she went down the steps and signaled to her dog, who had been lying on the walk in the sun.

Slug avoided me all morning long, going into the kitchen after I had cleaned up my breakfast dishes and gone upstairs, to the second floor when I was on the first, and out the back door when I was coming in the front. We somehow managed to occupy different parts of the house, each stepping around where the other might have been, or might want to go.

Just after noon, when I was in the cellar stuffing clothes into the washer, I looked up to see her sitting on the bottom step, her arms wrapped around her knees, her head tilted up while she studied the pipes in the ceiling as if they were markings on a map.

"It's okay," she said. "We could try letting her go home. Taking care of her. If you still want."

I moved a box of soap powder off a chair and sat down facing her. "Are you sure? No reservations?"

"No, I'm not sure. And with all kinds of reservations."

"Me, too," I said. "We would need help. It's a big undertaking. But there're Ernestus Stokes and Mattie-Miller already.

"It'll be draining; emotionally, I mean. Watching her get progressively worse."

"Yeah," said Slug, and I couldn't help wondering if this was the way she had talked before, in the parts of her life I didn't know about. Yes. No. Maybe. So.

"Okay, I'll get back to Ernestus Stokes and Mattie-Miller, and give Mr. Bigelow a try, but I'm doubtful there. I'll talk to the social worker and see if there's any support system from the hospital. How about David Norton and his parents?"

"David, yes. I'm sure. He's terribly in awe of Miss Tegges as an artist and he likes her, too. But I don't know about his parents. He hasn't said much, but I get the feeling that things aren't terrific there." She stood and started up the steps.

"You talk to David, then, and I'll tackle his mother and father—we won't put him in the middle of that one. Oh, and Slug, you're not going along with this for me, are you?"

She turned, hanging over the banister and looking down at me. "It's not for you at all."

I winced at that one.

"It's—I guess you could say it's for Gussie," said Slug. "But most of all it's for Miss Tegges."

"Yes," I said. "Let's just say it's for Harper Tegges."

After she had left I turned on the washer and stood looking into it, watching it fill with water, the agitator grinding back and forth. I felt, oddly enough, that we were even. Starting off on the same foot. Okay, Slug, I thought. Okay, Mary Rose October, let's take it from here.

Harper

I'M HOME. Not that I came home on my own, with all my working parts, mind you. No. They carried me flat out on a stretcher. In an ambulance. The beached whale again.

"I want to go home," I said.

"Nursing home," somebody said. "Nursing home. Nursing home. Take care of you."

I don't care for that idea. I don't care, I tell you. I told them. I don't give a damn.

They brought me home, and now my house has been overrun. By a plague of locusts. They cluster there, hanging on to tree trunks and in the bushes. In my studio, dangling from the walls and window frames. Rubbing their legs together. Making noise.

Just until. Until what? Until I'm on my feet again. Can do for myself. Can work: paint. Because work is all. Until. Until. Oh, Christ. Until I die.

But I won't. Not yet. I'll fool them. Make a deal. Let them into my house. All of them—Julie and Slug and Ernestus Stokes. David from next door and Mattie-

Miller and— That's all. Nobody's mentioned the butcher and his wimp wife. Or the other one. The old man with his garden. Mr.—what's his name? "Mary, Mary, quite contrary, how does your garden grow." Mr. Bigelow. He's old and if I die he'll be scared shitless. But I won't. I'll fool them all.

Maybe Mama'll come. And Aunt Agnes—she was the caretaker of the family. The one who came with her tisanes and mustard plasters.

Richard. Suzanne. She can't, can she? She doesn't know who I am, I don't think. Did Richard ever tell—

I'm muddled now. Things are muddled and there's a pain in my head. I have to go slow.

"Do you want to go home, Miss Tegges? To your own home?"

Who said that? A—a social worker. Whatever. "Your neighbors have said—"

Julie was there. "It's up to you, Harper."

"Stop fussing, Harper. Aunt Agnes has come. She made chamomile tea. It's just the flu—the measles—chicken pox—a broken leg." Aunt Agnes smells stale and I don't like her.

Dr. Head Cutter was there. "Turning you over, Miss Tegges, to another doctor." Turning you over. A pancake. A mattress. A spadeful of earth. Digging. Digging. A hole. A grave. "Like a grave," I said, and Dr. Head Cutter looked where I wasn't and hurried out of the room. I was not one of his successes. And I wouldn't say thank you. I would not say it.

Mama would've. Mama always said thank you. A well-brought-up young lady remembers her manners.

Thanks for what?

Another doctor? Dr. Lynch should be here. He always was before. Old Dr. Lynch with his umbrella the size of a circus tent. He took care of all of us. The boys —Francis, Edwin, and John. And me. Papa and Mama, too. "Doctor Foster went to Gloucester/In a shower of rain;/He stepped in a puddle, up to his middle,/And never went there again."

When Suzanne was born she came so quickly. At home, in the house by the field, with only Richard there, and the woman from down the road. And now you've created something, Harper my girl, I said. But it wasn't enough.

What I think is—when I *can* think—I'll let them come into my house, into my studio, just until I'm well again.

Sometimes the thoughts scatter, then crowd together like dustballs under a bed. Under something in my head. My head with the hair all gone but, I can feel it, bristling back again. Ugly.

They're here. And I'm here. In my studio, so that now it looks like that Klee painting *Room Perspective with Occupants*—all lines and angles and shades of brown.

I close my eyes and see my own room in perspective. Going back. Fitted out with a bed with buttons that make it go up and down, like in the hospital. A proper bed. My easels . . . my canvases . . .

Occupants. Julie and the rest.

And Ginger. Asleep on the foot of my bed. I'm glad about that.

Slug

ONCE I said that I would help her with Harper Tegges it was as if Julie took hold of my giving in and ran with it, just like Miss Tegges's dog, Ginger, when she grabbed her red rubber ball and tore around the yard with *it*. I guess I couldn't have changed my mind even if I'd wanted to.

I was learning that Julie was like that. She had a way of attacking things that she wanted to do. And now it looked like Miss Tegges was going to be a buffer between us the same way working on that swing had been. But that was okay with me. All my life I'd wanted to know about Julie, and now suddenly I knew too much. More than I could handle: piles and piles of Julie-facts stacked around me like Gussie's treasures. The only trouble was that none of them was what I'd wanted it to be.

There had always been things I'd wanted to know —but who my father was wasn't one of them. It wasn't until I actually met Julie that I began seeing her as

maybe half of a couple. Before that time it had only
been my mother that I thought about: Where was she
and was she coming back? Would she like me? The
thing is that *my* not knowing who my father was didn't
seem nearly as bad as *Julie's* not knowing.

Julie—like that—made me think of Candy Mae
Kane from my class at school. Of course her real name
was Hanna Mae instead of Candy Mae, but all you ever
heard around school, up and down the halls, by the
water fountains and in line at the cafeteria was that
"Hanna Mae was everybody's Candy Cane and you
know what they're good for." Then there was the
graffiti: on the sides of the gym lockers, along the
downstairs hall by the biology lab, and even in the girls'
bathroom—I never figured that one out. Stuff like,
"It's dandy with Candy—555-1464," or "Want a
piece of Candy?—555-1464." It got so that after a
while everybody in school knew Hanna Mae Kane's
phone number whether they wanted to or not. It
wasn't gossip, either—I mean everybody *knew*. Last
year when we went on our class trip to Williamsburg
and Sue Ellen Chase and Mary Warren had to share a
room with her, they were afraid they'd get something.
From towels and stuff.

I've always had this picture of Julie in my mind: tall
and thin with long blond hair. It was unrealistic, sort
of, and I guess that deep down I knew she didn't look
like those old pictures of Grace Kelly. It was her inside
self that was important, and the way I thought of Julie,

she could have looked like Attila the Hun and it wouldn't have mattered.

Maybe I should have known better, because in that whole town nobody ever said to me, "I remember your mother and she was one terrific person." Not Mrs. Lynam next door, or old pinch-faced Mrs. Prather, who taught me part of sixth grade until Miss Albright came (even though I asked her once point-blank). Not Dr. Mercy, who is one of the most up-front people I know; not Mr. Trimper, or Mrs. Trimper, or Mrs. Caldwell at the library (never "Oh, those were the books your mother used to like," and she'd been there long enough to know what Betsy Ross liked—if Betsy Ross had lived in our town). And certainly not Gussie. Never Gussie. And it wasn't because I didn't ask. I asked all the time—and everybody—so that now, looking back, it makes my skin crawl. *Especially* now, when it turns out that Julie, my mother, was the Candy Mae Kane of her class. I wonder what they wrote on the bathroom walls about her.

The thing is, I never thought very much about sex. Well, that's a lie. Of course I thought about it. All the time. Back when Miss Albright married Jason Burton, when we were in seventh grade, and we all got to go to the wedding at the Presbyterian church, and afterward the girls in our class went back to Henley's house for something to eat because we weren't invited to the reception. During that whole time we kept talking and giggling and carrying on. "Do you think they've done it yet?" and "How many times?" and "Do people really *like* it?" Afterward, when everybody'd gone home, I spent the night with Henley (because we were best friends by then) and she tiptoed down and got one of Dr. Mercy's medical books. Actually that was pretty boring, but we kept reading, waiting to get to the good part; only after a while we figured we had gone right past it and not even known it. It was all so anatomical. Then Dr. Mercy came in and wanted to know what we were doing. Henley always said that when Dr. Mercy wanted to know something you just found yourself telling her. Henley dragged the book out from under the bed, and Dr. Mercy took us down to the kitchen and made cocoa and said that for people our age (she could say that without making it sound like there was anything *wrong* with our age) it was best not to learn about sex from a medical book. It might make it all sound so "prohibitive" (that was the word she used). She talked on and on about sex and caring and how the caring part was really what mattered, and did we have any questions? We didn't really. At least not any we wanted to ask—but we felt we could have.

The caring part was what Brian talked about one time when he was down. He asked me to go for a walk and he talked all about love and sex: how it was a ter-rific thing but how you should be sure, not indiscrim-inate. Poor Brian. I think Gussie kind of stored up these things for him to talk to me about when he came to visit. Summer jobs; flunking math; the note from

Mrs. Prather that said I daydreamed a lot; sex. I guess you could say Gussie put these things on hold. She might have gotten to the job or math or even daydreaming if Brian hadn't come, but I'm pretty sure Gussie wouldn't have talked about sex.

Anyway, what I mean when I say I never thought too much about it is I just always figured that someday there'd be somebody who really mattered a lot to me and then—then everything'd be okay. Not "prohibitive," as Dr. Mercy said. But not "indiscriminate," either. Probably the whole time Brian and I were walking around town, over by the school and down by the beach, along Main Street, what he wanted to say was "Just don't be like your mother, kid." Only he never did.

But now, thinking about Julie makes me feel dirty. So much so that even remembering the times, back home, when I was with Wally Jones—at the movies or parties or things like that—and he held my hand or put his arms around me or kissed me, I feel dirty in retrospect. There's something else that bothers me too: if Julie was what she was, and if I was the result of what she was, what does that make me? And somehow the things that Dr. Mercy and Brian said seem very far away. I'm not even sure I'll *ever* want any part of them.

Julie was throwing herself into getting ready for Miss Tegges to come home. She talked to the social worker and learned that the hospital had a team that worked with patients who were terminally ill and wanted to die at home. And because Miss Tegges needed someone with her all the time, she made out a schedule for Ernestus Stokes, Mattie-Miller, David, herself, and me, and a list of phone numbers to call for this, that, or the other thing. Apparently when Julie asked David's mother if she would be able to help, Mrs. Norton said yes, but thought up seventy-nine reasons why she couldn't right now. And Mr. Norton just went on about how that's what happened to artists and what did she expect: that she should have provided for "any eventuality." I had a mental picture of Miss Tegges as a squirrel storing away caretakers. As for Mr. Bigelow—when Julie talked to him he didn't even answer. Just harrumphed and hemmed and hawed and turned back to the bushes he was trimming.

By the time Miss Tegges came home, Julie had everything arranged: schedules in multiples—one for each of us and one stuck to the front of Miss Tegges's refrigerator door; a hospital bed; pans and basins and medicine bottles. To give her credit, she kept things out of the way as much as possible so that, except for the hospital bed in the middle of things, it didn't look too much like a sickroom. But even with all Julie's arrangements I had cold feet the first time I had to go and stay with Miss Tegges by myself.

It was one of those settled-in-to-rain summer days, the kind where all you want to do is curl up and read a book somewhere just close enough to a window so a small damp wind blows against your face. It was a Saturday and I knew Julie had plans to meet a friend downtown, but even so I couldn't help wishing that she was going to be home all afternoon. In case something went wrong. In case I needed her. I mean, just me and Miss Tegges. It scared me.

I stood for a minute on the front porch, looking across the street. The wind came in gusts, and from down at the streambed I heard the sudden roar of water. It sounded ominous. Crouching into my slicker, I pulled the hood over my head and ran.

Julie met me at the door, raising her eyebrows and saying under her breath, "It hasn't been a good day. She's angry and—" Then out loud: "Good. Come on in. Miss Tegges is waiting for you. Hang your coat in the kitchen."

It seemed that I had just gotten there and Julie was putting on her own coat and picking up her book. "I've got to run to get downtown by one, but Miss Stokes will be here by suppertime and she said she'll be home most of the afternoon if you have any problems. Oh, and don't forget the list of phone numbers by the telephone." I watched her stop at the bed, and when Miss Tegges didn't open her eyes, I saw Julie touch the woman's hand before she moved quickly across the room and out the door.

And suddenly, with Julie's going, the walls of the house seemed to stretch outward, surrounding me with empty space, as if Miss Tegges and I were at opposite ends of a tunnel. I looked across at her: at the hospital bed with the dog curled at the foot, the commode pushed slightly to one side, the bedside table, bare except for a lamp and a paperweight with snow heaped around a pine tree. I wanted to go after Julie, grab my slicker and run back across the street. Rain lashed the windows and my thoughts spun inside my head. I didn't want to be here alone with Miss Tegges. She might get sick, really sick. Throw up. She might need a bedpan. Fall out of bed. Or die. I wiped a film of cold sweat off my forehead. Outside, the wind seemed to shift, driving the rain against the house from a different direction. I took a deep breath, and another one. I moved into the kitchen to the little television set on the counter, turning it on so that I had just the picture and no sound, watching the Orioles play in pantomime.

"I'm not asleep, and if I were, all that pussy-footing around would give me the screaming whim-whams." At the sound of Miss Tegges's voice I looked up, surprised to see the room back to its normal size and shape. I turned away from the TV as she went on to say, " 'A good firm footstep,' Mama used to say. That and a good firm handshake were what she looked for in people. People maybe, but not her daughter, of course. And when I used that good firm footstep to get the hell away from there—"

Miss Tegges picked up the paperweight from the table and threw it, all in one gesture. It seemed to stop in midair, the snow inside tumbling wildly, change direction, and fall to the floor just past the foot of the bed.

"You missed," I said, moving toward her, planting my feet firmly on the floor and stooping to pick up the paperweight.

"Did not. I wasn't aiming," she said, opening and closing her fingers. "You can't miss if you weren't aiming, can you?"

With that I stuck my hand out, catching at Miss Tegges's and shaking it up and down. "A good firm handshake," I said.

"Did your mother say that, too?"

"No. Yours did. Anyway, for me it was Gussie. Remember?" I stood for a minute holding on to her hand before I said, "And Gussie didn't go in much for saying things like that."

But Miss Tegges was pulling her hand away and holding it out in front of her as she tried to squeeze it into a fist. "Good for nothing."

"It's rough, isn't it?" I said, not at all sure what I should be saying.

"Shit," said Miss Tegges.

"But maybe—"

"Don't 'maybe' me," she said, rubbing her left hand over her stubbly hair while her other hand lay open in her lap. "Maybe what? Maybe, maybe, maybe. Maybe this hand'll take off on its own. Drawing. Painting. Shit." She closed her eyes and didn't say any more.

After a while I eased myself backward away from the bed. Just as I was about to pick up my book I heard Miss Tegges speak. "I have to get up," she said, thrashing her legs back and forth so that Ginger stood up, stretched, and jumped onto the floor.

I waited, scarcely moving, not sure whether she was talking to me or not.

"I have to get up," Miss Tegges said again, her head and shoulders rocking forward. "There's something I have to do. I have to—"

And I was standing beside her bed, my hands hovering just above her, willing her back. "Hey, wait a minute, Miss Tegges. Maybe you should—I should— I could call Miss Stokes."

"Now," she said. "I have to do it now." She swung herself forward so that her legs dangled over the side of the bed.

"Wait. What is it you want? I'll get it—"

Miss Tegges waved her hand to the back of the studio. "There—on the easel. Get it."

For a minute I wavered there, afraid to leave her alone, afraid not to go. "You want the picture? You want me to bring it to you?"

"I have to finish it," she said, measuring her words out evenly. "There's something else . . ."

I looked down at her: at the way her cheekbones bulged against the skin under her eyes, the way her right hand curved as if she were holding something. I put my hands carefully on Miss Tegges's shoulders

and eased her back onto the pillows. "Okay. Just promise me you won't move and I'll bring it to you. Wait
right here." And I went across the studio, dodging
empty easels, rocking chairs, and tables piled with
brushes and paints and jars. I lifted the painting off,
leaning it against the wall, and picked up the easel,
moving with it toward Miss Tegges as if I were making
my way across a dance floor with a reluctant partner.
Putting the painting back on the easel, I turned to
face her.

"Chair," she said, after looking at it for a long time.
"And a palette, and the brushes. There by the window.
I need a tube of red paint, the one marked alizarin
crimson, I think. And burnt umber, too. Oh, and linseed oil for the brushes." Her eyes burned with a kind
of fervor as she watched me moving around the room.

When everything was together she let her head drop
back, and for a minute I thought she had gone to sleep.
Then after a while she spoke, opening her eyes and
seeming to gather herself together so that she suddenly
looked more compact there on the bed. "To the chair
first, I think."

I wasn't at all sure that Miss Tegges should be doing
this, but somehow I knew that it would be worse if she
didn't do it. "Okay," I said. "Just tell me what you
want me to do." She gestured for me to come and stand
beside her, reaching for my arm as she slid off the bed
and stood, swaying for a moment, before she shuffled
over to the chair. Her hand against my arm felt light

and brittle. When I had her settled in the captain's chair in front of the easel, she tilted sharply to one side, so that I had to hold on to her shoulders while I reached backward for pillows, stuffing them behind her.

Miss Tegges sat there, fighting to hold her head up, looking at the painting. There was a slight sound and I turned to see David Norton standing by the front door, rainwater running off his poncho and dripping onto the floor. He moved quietly toward the kitchen, peeling off the wet plastic, as if by saying anything he might upset Miss Tegges's fragile balance.

"Now," she said. She nodded to the palette and I held it out to her, turning my eyes away as she fumbled on the table for a tube of paint. Out of the corner of my eye I saw a blob of thick red paint, saw it darken as she added brown from the other tube. I felt the pressure on the palette as she blended one into the other.

"Now," she said again, sucking in a breath that seemed to come from her feet. "I have to stand."

And somehow I knew to put the palette down on the table. Knew to move around in back of her, lifting until she was part-standing and part-leaning, and I could feel her bones sharp against my chest.

Another breath. Her arm lifted and the brush stroked across the canvas, which was already filled with things I saw as if from far away: a letter of a sort; meat hanging—sausages; porch spindles; flowers all in a row; a dog, and this selfsame picture as it was repeated low and to the front. And what looked to me like the shadow of a girl; only Miss Tegges had said there wasn't any girl.

The new paint glistened wet and seemed to draw the whole thing together. The line was more than a line: a petal, a stem, a thorn.

Miss Tegges sighed and slumped against me, and David came suddenly forward, picking her up, and putting her back in bed with the brush still held tightly in her hand.

I waited until her fingers had slackened, then took the brush away from her, and David cleaned it with turpentine. Then we stood in front of the painting, backing off and moving in close again. And all the time that I looked, it was as if something darted just beyond my grasp. Still without saying anything, we moved over to the living room.

"It gave me chills, watching Miss Tegges do whatever she did to her painting," I said. "Almost like—"

"Like what?" said David, coming to sit next to me on the daybed and picking up an oval of marble from the table, rubbing it gently with his hands.

"I started to say like we were a part of it. But anyway, if it gives me chills like that, I can just imagine what it does to you."

"Yeah," said David. "But do you realize that that might be the last painting she works on? It's not fair."

"But look at all she *has* done."

"I guess. But there could have been so much more if only—that damn tumor."

"There could always be more, I guess," I said, leaning back and stretching my legs out in front of me. "But at least she knew what she wanted to do—and she did it. If you ask me, there's nothing worse than not having done *anything*. That's where you're so lucky, knowing what you have to do. And Henley, too."

"Who's Henley?"

"My friend in Virginia; she's going to be a writer. I mean, there's absolutely no way she's *not* going to be one. It's the same feeling I get with you. Vibes I guess you could say, except I hate that word."

"Yeah, but I wish my parents'd get them. The vibes, I mean. Do you know they won't even come over here and help with taking care of Miss Tegges. It's one excuse after another. Wonderful neighbors, aren't they?"

"Is it that they don't like her, or they don't know her, or—"

"It's her. They don't like her *and* they don't *know* her. How d'you like them apples? You should've been around when they heard she was moving in next door. My father stalked around the house calling her that damn artist in the way he says that damn nigger, Commie, fag, wop—you name it.

"You want to know something," David went on, putting the piece of marble firmly back on the table.

"I think one of the things that blew his mind about my wanting to paint (my God, chimps in the zoo paint pictures) is that I might be gay. I mean, in my father's mind artist equals gay. My son the fag. I'm not, by the way," he said, looking across at me.

"I know," I said. "Vibes again, I guess." And we each made a face and laughed.

After a minute David got up and went over to the bookcase along one wall, running his fingers down the spines of the books. "I'll never forget the first time I came in here. Miss Tegges needed some help uncrating something and she asked me. I guess she saw the way I was looking at her paintings, at the books, at the whole studio. Kind of like the way my friend Eric looks at the inside of Corky's liquor store—like he wants to swallow it all down at once. I remember she let me take home a book about Michelangelo that day and told me to keep it as long as I wanted and when I was finished to come back and get another one. I kept Michelangelo for a month, traded him for Leonardo, then back to Michelangelo. Brueghel, and Michelangelo again. She started giving me the more modern painters—some of her favorites. Miró. Klee. Chagall. Kandinsky. I'd've given anything to have talked about those books, but we never did. I guess it was all a part of the way she kept herself from being distracted."

I looked over at him standing in front of the bookcase, his hands shoved down into his jeans pockets, and then I moved over to check on Miss Tegges, who was still sleeping soundly. When I came back I said, "There's one thing I don't understand. Why you stay —at home, I mean. If they don't like what you do and you don't like—"

"Money," said David, coming back to sit beside me. "And how I don't have any—what with tuition and books, insurance for my car, art supplies."

"Don't your parents help, I mean with the tuition and all?"

"Oh, they would have. If I'd agreed to major in accounting or something practical. But I refused and they refused. So now I work summers, and part-time during the school year at Sloane's garage, and old man Sloane throws in the room over the garage for me to use as a studio for not much rent. My father says the smell of paint gives him asthma. Asthma, for god's sake. He's never wheezed in his life," he said. "Oh well, one more year of college and I can be on my own. But enough about me. Tell me about you—what it is you want to do."

"I'm not sure," I said.

"But you have an idea?" said David, looking right at me.

"I've never said this out loud before, and it seems kind of crazy, since I'm not wild about hospitals and sick people scare me some, but sometimes I think I want to be a doctor. One like Dr. Mercy, though, not like Miss Tegges's Dr. Chickenshit. At least that's what Julie calls him."

I looked at David. He was nodding his head up and down as if it made all the sense in the world for me to be thinking past college and on to medical school. And the funny thing was, when I said it out loud, the whole idea didn't seem as impossible as it had before.

Just at that moment we heard Miss Tegges calling and moved over to her. We stood watching as she plucked at the front of her nightgown and the covers on her bed, a low noise coming from her throat, like an animal in pain. As we watched, she took up the paperweight again. This time when it arced just beyond the foot of the bed and fell to the floor, I let it lie there, and together we turned away, as if from something we should not have seen. David went over and turned up the television, but all that we heard was the sound of Miss Tegges's voice, which seemed to fill all the spaces of the room.

Harper

THE PAINTING is done. My street scene. Slug, who is Mary Rose. And she was here. Held me up. And David, too. Lifted me back to bed, I think. The first time he came, there was something that needed doing. A crate—a box. And he stood, his eyes wide at what he saw here. I sent him home with Michelangelo. Not bad company that.

But now there's more. Paintings I haven't—not done yet—

And the canvases—the blank ones all around me. Taunting me. Ha-ha-ha. You can't catch me. I'm the gingerbread boy— Ha-ha-ha. You can't—

I shake my fist at it all, only my fist waves—jerks.

There's more. Please. The show at the—at the museum— I think. Someplace. So much more. If only— And me. Me. I want— If only I could go on being who I am. Not—

Julie

"IT'S A good thing there's no traffic to speak of on this street or David would lose his feet," I said, nodding to the orange Pinto and David Norton's feet sticking out from under it.

"Mmmmm," said Slug. She was sitting on Harper's front steps, a book open on her knees, but instead of reading she was watching a ladybug walk back and forth across the pages. "I'm glad you're here," she said as I settled onto the step beside her.

"Is it getting to you, being here with Harper?"

"A little," said Slug. Then after a minute: "A lot, I guess. I mean, I'm glad she's home and all. And it's not even the way she's getting bony and caved-in-looking that bothers me so much." She slammed the book, letting out a little cry as she scrabbled to open it. "The ladybug," she said, poking at a reddish blot on the page. Suddenly tears rolled down her face.

"Hey, come on now," I said, reaching out and patting at the air in front of her, not quite touching her, and thinking that I was seeing some inside part of Slug

I'd never seen before. "It's only a— No, it's not that, is it? Not the ladybug at all."

Slug sniffed and darted her tongue out, catching at tears as they ran past either side of her mouth. "It's today, the way she's just sitting there. Slumped but still strapped into that chair you got for her. Not saying a word. And the thing about it is that Mattie-Miller took the folding screen in the studio and covered it all over with pictures from magazines and old greeting cards of puppies and kittens and stuff like that." She hiccupped and went on. "And you just *know* that Miss Tegges's got to think it's mud-fence ugly. It's the kind of thing she would hate, only she doesn't *say* anything. That screen is there, kind of hovering over her, and looking as large as it ever did—and she hasn't even *thrown* anything at it."

"Not even the paperweight?" I said, trying to be funny in the very way I *hate* for people to try to be funny, as if the person with you wasn't hurting at all. But somehow the idea of Slug's crying bothered me. I had never thought of her crying before. In all those seventeen years when I had tried to think what she might be doing, what she might be like, it had always been a happy child I saw. Slug at a birthday party, in swimming, on the Ferris wheel at the firemen's carnival. Going on hayrides and to picnics on the beach, to a dance at the high school. And now, for the first time, I knew it hadn't been like that.

"Not even the paperweight," she said, answering me

more seriously than I had spoken. "I thought I told you, that went during the week. Hit the wall and the dome came off, splattering water and soggy snowflakes every which way. Same as the two spoons, a medicine glass, a bran muffin, and a vase of roses David's mother sent over. But that makes some kind of sense. At least I can understand her being angry, but now it's as if the fight's gone out of her, like air going out of a balloon."

"I think she's depressed," I said. I was getting to be a real master at stating the obvious.

"I guess," said Slug, waving to David as he crawled out from under the car and stood wiping his hands on the seat of his pants. "But it's—oh, I don't know. Weird. Not comfortable. Spooky, sort of. I mean, you talk and she doesn't answer. You don't talk and she still doesn't say anything, and after a while the silence just piles up around you. That's what I'm doing out here—I thought maybe she wanted to be by herself. But I don't really know *what* she wants."

I watched as David came up the walk, calling to Slug. "If you've finished here, come on and I'll take you over to the garage, show you my *Feet on Canvas*. Okay if I take her away?" he asked, turning to me.

And his asking that made me feel inadequate, as if I were some kind of impostor mother who should have the answers to all kinds of things I didn't know about. I stood quickly, moving up a step to make myself taller, and said, "Sure. It'd be good for her to get away for a bit. Oh, and David, be sure and thank your mother for those roses—" I felt a laugh churning somewhere inside of me and tried to swallow it back, biting down on my lip. I heard Slug start to snicker and couldn't look at her.

"Yeah," said David. "I heard my mom picked some roses and sent them over. Heard it from two directions and in stereo. It really freaked my father out, but since it was probably her first independent act I hope Miss Tegges enjoyed them."

"Oh, she did, she certainly did," said Slug, choking and gasping, laughing so hard that she had to lean against him. "I'll tell you just how she enjoyed them on the way, but first there's something I have to do for Miss Tegges."

"Okay," said David. "I'll meet you by the car."

Slug followed me into the house, and I knew what she meant as soon as we walked through the door. Even as I blinked at the darkness of the room after the sunlight outside, I felt the silence layered all around me. I heard it in contrast to the sounds of water dripping in the kitchen sink and the thump of Ginger's tail against the floor.

Harper sat, as if in a pocket of quiet, huddled in her chair. Her head, stubbled now with new hair, hung forward, her chin resting on her chest. She drummed her fingers soundlessly on the tray in front of her.

"Hi," I said, sitting on the edge of the bed and waiting for my eyes to adjust to the light. "It's nice out there today." Someone had moved the little television over closer to the bed, putting it on a stool. "Good day for a ball game," I said, looking at it. I laughed a little but let it go quickly, like releasing the string of a balloon. "Maybe later on we could go out on the porch. I'll slide you right along in that chair."

Harper looked past me and I turned to see Slug clearing off the folding screen. She worked quickly, unfastening pins and shoving the pictures down into the trash can: all those puppies in boxes and baskets and peeking out of paper bags; kittens tangled in skeins of wool and chasing cellophane.

When she was finished she stood back, as if surprised at what she had done and not at all sure what to do next.

"You go on. David'll be waiting," I said, taking hold of one side of the screen and folding it into the center.

"Okay—and thanks." She started toward the door, turned back to Harper, and said, "Oh, and Miss Tegges, I'm off to see David's *Feet on Canvas!*"

When I came back from putting the screen down in the basement, Harper was drumming her fingers on the tray again, this time making a sound like the hooves of distant horses.

"That's better, isn't it?" I said. "Now the air can circulate—it won't be so warm in here for you. I mean, just because we're all coming in and out of the house, things are still up to you. You do know that, don't you?"

I was beginning to feel like a comedian who couldn't make the audience laugh. Sitting down on the edge of the bed, I tried to think of something else to say or do. It was then I noticed that someone had pushed the easel, with the painting Slug had held Harper up to finish, off to the side, and I went to it, pulling it closer, angling it toward the bed. I stood, my hand on the back of a rocking chair, looking at the jumble of empty easels, Harper's paints and brushes, her canvases leaning against the walls. And it was as if I had to finish something Slug had started when she untrimmed the screen. I picked up an easel, carried it back, and went for another one. I spaced them just beyond the foot of the bed. I looked at Harper, waiting for a minute to see if I was on the right track, but when there was no change in her I hurried back to the studio, flipping through canvases, pulling out paintings and propping them up.

I chose pictures where the colors were bright and bold and seemed to draw me in. For a minute I stood staring at all the lines and shapes, not sure exactly what they meant but somehow liking them, the freedom and the feeling of movement. I picked up one—yellows and blues and reds, black darting lines, on a background that went from brown into green; and then another—yellow, with heads, bits of what could be stick people. In both of them it was as if there was an unnamed something that floated just beyond my understanding. Carrying them back, I put them on the easels and moved to stand at the head of Harper's bed so that I could see them the way she would see them. I shoved the bed over a little until it was centered, surrounded by work that she had done.

When I looked at Harper, she was sitting with her head still hanging to the side, but her fingers were now quiet on the table. Then I went to her, fumbling with the strap that fastened her into the chair, talking as I supported her back into bed. "There now," I said. "And we can change them any time you say. Put others up. Is this okay? Is it all right?" And for one crazy moment I saw again the posters and signs that had been on the walls of all the apartments Monica and I had lived in in New York: TAKE A HIPPIE TO LUNCH; FLOWER POWER; TURN ON TUNE IN DROP OUT; VIVE L'AMOUR. Oh, God, I thought. So long ago, so like yesterday. I blinked and looked again—at Harper's paintings looking back at me.

Harper rested her head on the mound of pillows propped up on the bed. She closed her eyes, then opened them, looking at the paintings, while, unawares, her left hand kneaded the fingers of her right. She sat up abruptly, waving toward the bookcase at the front of the room. A terrible exhaustion seemed to have taken hold of me, and in spite of Harper's now frantic gesturing I couldn't move. Finally her hands dropped onto her chest. She rubbed her head and shook it slowly. "I'd like a book," she said, once more stabbing her fingers in the air. "Miró, I think. Klee— and Chagall."

I brought the books, carrying them one at a time and putting them down on the bed next to her. I watched her pick one up, lay it on her lap, and open it, turning the pages almost without seeing them. When she got to where she wanted to be, she looked down at the painting. Then she put her head back, closing her eyes and stroking the page with her fingers. It was such a physical thing that I had to step away, going to stand by the front door, watching the way the sunlight filtered through the trees onto the street.

The way I had remembered those posters from my old apartments had jolted me, setting me adrift, and for a minute I was in New York, in Virginia again. I was with Gussie, Monica, my brother Brian. With the Slug-baby and all the boys and men I had ever known. I found myself holding on to the screen door, digging into it until my fingers whitened around the knuckles.

When I was in high school I didn't look the way I wanted to look and it mattered more than anything had ever mattered to me before. And what was worse was that the way I didn't look covered up an emptiness inside, a me-ness that wasn't there. Sometimes in the afternoons I would stand in Gussie's kitchen, looking into the broken piece of mirror over the sink at my wiry dark hair, which frizzed around my head as if pull-

ing away at the roots from a face that was just a face,
not at all like the faces on the covers of the magazines
in the drugstore racks downtown. Then I would move
back, bumping against the table, looking at my body,
which was flat and sharp-edged in all the wrong places;
up onto the kitchen table, which swayed from side to
side but let me see my spindle legs and knob-like knees.
Gussie-legs, I thought one time as I watched her coming down the street, dragging that damn red wagon.
And all the times after that, whenever I saw her going
through the streets and alleys of town, it was as if some
shadow part of myself was going along with her. She
was a freak and I was a freak, and on the night that
three of the boys in the ninth grade came to the
Halloween party in the school gym dressed as my
mother I ran all the way home, as if what was chasing
me was coming along behind, instead of locked inside
me. And I didn't go back until the school home visitor
came after me the following week.

There had been a book once that Brian and I read
at the library, before I stopped going to the library
because Mrs. Caldwell was all the time telling me to
use a Kleenex and to go and wash my hands—*The
Ugly Duckling*. I asked Gussie about it once, standing
in the middle of the front room floor with her day's
haul spread out around me. Asked her if my hair would
grow long and smooth and my skin would be like roses.
I twirled around and fell against an orange crate and

waited for her to say that, to her, I was already a swan. But she laughed, rocking back in her chair, and held a peacock feather up to the light.

That's the way I remembered it, anyway. But maybe I was wrong. Maybe the Gussie who raised me wasn't the Gussie who raised Slug—or Brian, either. Because what I know now is that we all change. We all bring different things to different people.

But in that time long ago there was only one thing I wanted, and that was for somebody, somewhere, to like me, to want me. And I found a way.

It started with a party that was more than a party— a class project, really, at the end of ninth grade. Mrs. Waters, our homeroom teacher, talked on and on a blue streak about how we were going to do it all: planning, ordering, cooking, cleaning up. There was a committee for everything. "You'll learn by doing," she said. And some of us did. I wonder if she ever knew how much.

We had the party up at Leggets beach, five miles north of town, getting rides from some of the parents, who, except for the ones who were to be chaperones, dropped us off and came back for us later on. It was, after all, *our* evening. There was a fire on the beach that smoked and spit in the beginning, so the hot dogs were cold in the middle, but turned to a raging inferno in time for the marshmallow roast. There were relay races, and Frisbees flying through the air (the game committee, of course), and afterward, when the darkness settled down around us and the chaperones took a walk up the beach singing old songs and kicking at the water, there was a game of spin the bottle.

Billy Wilkins had a bottle of beer stashed away in the basket with the potato salad his mother had sent, and after he obligingly emptied it, he got to go first. Bottles don't spin well on sand, he found out, so that even with his poking and nudging it along, it stopped short: pointing at me instead of Flossie Moore. I heard them all groaning and laughing there in the circle as he pulled me, hurting my wrist, back behind the dune. But he had a faraway smile on his face when we came back, and afterward, when the chaperones returned and everybody got really interested in songs around the campfire, he led me off again, smiling that same funny smile and licking his lips so that just the tip of his tongue showed.

I remember sand and a kind of scuffling, breathing like I had never heard anyone breathe before, and a pain that lasted well into the following day. But the next week Billy took me out again. And after that so did his friends Andy and Warren and Bobby. Tom, Dick, and Harry.

I knew, deep down, why they did it. But sometimes, when I looked in the broken mirror over Gussie's sink or in the window of the Pop Shop down on Main Street, it seemed, just for a minute, that my hair was longer and smoother, my skin more like roses.

I went to parties and movies and dances—that was

the price they paid. And afterward—there was always an afterward—in back rooms, on back porches, and in the backs of cars. That was the price *I* paid.

And all the while I knew what they were saying, what they were writing on the bathroom walls.

Later on, even while the Slug-baby, whose father I wasn't sure about, was being born, I knew I had to get away. There had been little enough of me to begin with—and now it was as if what was left was in danger of being thrown away with the afterbirth.

I left because I couldn't stay. It was as if I had boxed myself in with the person they all thought they knew ("Call Julie—555–1112"), only they didn't know me at all. And what was worse, I didn't know myself. It was my last chance and I grabbed at it.

Maybe a stronger person could have stayed. Looked them in the eye. Changed. But I couldn't. Not me. Not then. Because there wasn't anyone to help.

I remember crying all the way to New York: for Slug and for myself. For who I was and who I wasn't. So that when I got to the city my eyes burned like coals and I had a headache.

Looking over at Harper to make sure she was all right, I pushed open the door and went outside, sitting down on the top step and leaning back against the rail. The street had a hot-summer feel to it, as if everyone had locked up and gone someplace without telling anyone else. I felt terribly alone.

But I like to be alone, I thought. Have liked it ever since I found I *could* be alone—and that the company was good. And I saw myself again, the way I had seen myself when I first got to New York—like that old red-and-blue canvas raft Gussie had scavenged from somebody's trash, dragging it home and mending it with patches out of a kit from Western Auto. Brian and I took it off to the beach. Sometimes the patches held. Sometimes they didn't.

In the years after I left home I came to see my life as that sagging blue raft that was constantly being put back together, if not by Gussie, then at least by all the people I met along the way.

Of course there was Monica, that first night in the deli, taking me on, with no questions asked. There was Monica over and over again: pinning a button on me that said I *am a human being: do not bend, fold, spindle, or mutilate*; walking in bare feet with me through a downpour in the park and sharing the sound of the rain; blowing bubbles and watching the colors in the sunlight; going with me to the Goodwill for clothes that weren't from Mr. Trimper's dry-goods store; and understanding that for a while I had to be totally predictable, conforming in my nonconformity.

There were other patches, too. Living and eating with great crowds of people and caring about them; sharing, briefly, in the care of someone's baby, and that baby holding his arms out to me; the first apartment I had by myself, and pulling up the old linoleum, sweeping the roaches out from under. The first man who was my friend—with no afterward; the nurse in Baltimore who said, "Go to it, Julie Wilgus," and the way I did.

And there were the things that tore at me, letting the air seep out: all the bad things that happened with Monica and the way I ran away; not going to Gussie sooner, or to Slug. Then the patches again: a note to my brother, finding the house here on Butternut Street and scrounging enough money for the down payment. Having Slug come home.

I checked my watch and got up. Inside, I poured a dose of the blue medicine into a glass and took it to Harper. She lay with her eyes closed, her fingers still playing over the open book.

For a while after that Harper went on pretty much the same, and if I hadn't known better I would have thought that the doctor had made a mistake. That Harper, if she was not going to get better, would at least remain the same. Maybe I just wanted to see her that way.

One day when I went to take care of her Mattie-Miller was waiting for me. "I just got her back in bed," she said, coming out onto the front porch to talk to me. She rubbed the back of her neck, then fanned herself so that the red curls bounced on her forehead. "It's getting so I can hardly manage her alone anymore—I almost had to call somebody to come and help."

"I guess we're going to have to be careful about getting her up—unless there are two of us here at the same time," I said.

Mattie-Miller let her smile sag. "I was knitting an afghan once, all in shades of pink," she said. "And Rex or Duke—one of the dogs, anyway—got it off the needles, and as fast as I tried to catch the stitches they unraveled even faster. That's what it's like with Miss Tegges. We work hard at taking care of her, but she's unraveling all the time. She's getting worse and— Oh dear, I can't help thinking maybe we're not taking good *enough* care of her. Maybe there's something else we should do. If only we could— Oh, I just don't know."

"It's hard, but even with doing the best we can, sometimes things just happen." I felt that I sounded just like Mattie-Miller herself and I turned away from the two of us. "I'm going in—d'you want me to tell her you said goodbye?"

I watched as she pulled her smile tight again. "Oh no, no indeed. I'll just run along and say my toodle-oos. Besides, I have to get my things. I'm working on a scrapbook of flower pictures for Miss Tegges. Just to cheer her up, you know. Just to— I guess it's silly but—" She ducked her head and hurried into the house.

It wasn't until Mattie-Miller had gathered up her scissors, paste, and magazines, stuffed them into a shopping bag, and gone that I heard the sound of the ball game. The television was still on the stool to the side of Harper's bed, the sound turned up, the picture jittering across the screen. *A high fly ball into center field—Bumbry's going for it—he's got it—and that retires the side— At the end of—*

"Don't tell me you've turned into a fan," I said, pulling a chair alongside the bed and adjusting the picture on the TV.

"Pissants," said Harper in a gravelly voice. "It was 'Indeedy-do and open wide' or those men running every which way and hitting at each other and—"

"Not at each other," I said. "At the ball." I kept talking, hoping to get her interested. After all, it was going to be a long summer—and there were a lot of ball games. "The Orioles are playing the Yankees today. In New York." *There it is—a line drive deep into left field and—* "That was Rick Dempsey—he's—"

"I told them I would go to New York," said Harper, snatching at the covers. "It was when they came to Baltimore for my graduation from the Maryland Institute. My bags were packed and we were at the train station ready to go back. They *thought* we were ready. And I sat right down on that big old suitcase with the stickers all over it from my brother Edwin's trip abroad and said I wasn't going." Harper closed her eyes, and for a minute she moved her lips with no sound coming out. I reached to turn down the TV.

" 'Don't be silly, Harper. Where do you think you're

going to go?' Mama never would make a scene, so she was chewing her tongue damn near to ribbons.

" 'To New York, Mama,' I said.

" 'We'll talk about it at home,' said Papa.

" 'I'm not going home. There's a train coming through here just after five o'clock and I'm—'

" 'Young ladies don't go off alone,' Mama said.

" 'I do. I do.'

" 'We'll talk about it at home.'

" 'I'm not going home.'

" 'Mr. Gladstone at the high school said he would give you a position teaching drawing to the—'

" 'I'd sooner *die*,' I told them. 'I'd sooner die. Die. Die.'

" 'Hush up, Harper.' Mama was tight-lipped. She didn't like scenes. I think I told you.

" 'Be sensible. Mama's upset. Now, if you'll just—' My brothers tried. But I just sat there and wouldn't move an inch. And when their train came through heading south, I let them go without me. I had to go on, don't you see that?" Harper reached out, her bony fingers pulling at my arm.

And oddly enough, I felt all Harper's mother's words scolding against my own lips. All at once I was her father, and her brothers leaving her sitting on her suitcase in the middle of the station. But more than any of them, I was Harper. Knowing that she had to go, and going.

Harper choked and coughed. I brought her water, waiting as she drank it and lay back on her pillows. Finally I said, "What did you do in New York?"

" 'I frightened a little mouse under the chair.' " She lapsed into a singsong. " 'Pussy cat, pussy cat, where have you been? I've been up to London to look at the queen. Pussy cat, pussy cat, what did you there? I frightened a little mouse under the chair.'

"I painted," she said, opening her eyes wide. "Oh, my God, I painted. And I went to school. And I worked at any mind-rotting job I could find so I could save the important part of myself. Guarding it like Miss Ella Savage down home guarded her virginity. I was a file clerk, a ribbon clerk, an artist's model sometimes. It was so cold. Did you know those studios were cold?" She crossed her arms in front of her chest and began to shiver. Suddenly she sat up straight. "I breathed in oil paint and linseed oil and turpentine, and made stretchers for my canvases out of crates I found in the alley out back."

Harper took big breaths, rolling her head back and arching her back. "I sang for my supper—I did anything. Everything."

And for a minute I thought how the "everything" Harper had done had been nothing like the "everything" I had done, but her voice was going on and I had to catch up.

"Papa sent money once. Just once. I was living on West Twelfth Street then and I took that check and tore it up, flushed it down the toilet in the bathroom. I didn't ever want to be able to use that money. No money, no strings.

"And the work got better. Better. Except for the times when it didn't. Splitch-splotching across the page. Chicken scratchings. Gone. Tear up the paper. Start again. Begin again, begin again.

"None of us had any money, but we had more. Something. Jackson Pollock worked for the WPA. And Willem de Kooning. The WPA. Do you know what that was?" Harper asked, looking straight at me.

"I remember it from school—when we learned about the Depression," I said, not saying that I learned about it afterward, that I didn't learn *anything* in school except what I would have been better for not knowing ("You'll learn by doing," Mrs. Waters had said). But Harper was waving my words away as if she were clearing a room of smoke. She went on. "I had a painting in a show. In a gallery on the East Side. Another and another and another, until I had a show all to myself. And after that again. 'I knew a man named Michael Finnegan and he had whiskers on his chinigin. Begin again.'

"And the thirties were gone." Harper held her hand up, jerking it at the wrist as she tried to snap her fingers, and watched as they knotted into a fist instead. "We were at war and out of war. And still the work went on. I had a studio by then, with a skylight spotted over with pigeon shit. A daybed and my Spanish rug.

And when I had painted myself out, I would stretch on it flat. A beached whale indeed. All the time up until I went to California sometime in 1950, 1951—I can't remember. Everyone said— People had told me I had to go. Mama was sick by then, but I knew I wasn't ever going home. It didn't matter that they didn't understand. I didn't care. I *couldn't* care. Don't you see why I *had* to go?"

Harper pulled herself up, tugging on the metal sides of the bed that came down beside the pillows, hunching toward me and breathing sharp, rasping breaths.

"There has to be something that I've left behind. Some kind of a mark. Tell me, have I left something?"

"Yes, Harper. Yes," I said.

And she fell back, stroking her right hand, cradling it, crooning to it.

Harper

"Do you understand, Richard?" I asked him over and over. Asked someone. Meant to ask. It all runs together now. My brothers. Mama. Papa. Richard and Suzanne.

Paintings all around me. Inside and out. Whose? Mine? I can't be sure. It's all together now—paints on a palette.

My head hurts with things pulling this way and that. Coming and going.

People leave. Have to leave.

Do you understand, Richard?

Did you ever understand?

There was California, and on to Puget Sound. Richard. Richard. Richard. Richard.

Time lost and I never made it up again, and now there isn't any more. Won't be any more anything except the paintings in my head. I see them there, so real I reach for them. Touch them.

Christ.

Please.

Slug

JULIE WAS sitting at the kitchen table when I came in. I kicked off my sandals and watched as they skidded across the floor, hit the wall, and turned, facing back toward me. "She's impossible," I said.

"Who?" said Julie, looking up from the newspaper.

"Ernestus Stokes. You told me once about how the mailman told you she had a brother and he ran away. Well, all I can say is no *wonder*."

"He didn't *run* away. I mean, he was a grown man at the time. There must have been some kind of a disagreement and—"

"Oh, right. I forgot. Grownups don't run away, do they?" I said, almost daring her to tell me to shut up. Right about then a fight would've felt good.

Instead, she bit down on her lip and stared at the paper in front of her, so that I could feel her trying to be patient. After a while she said, "Was there trouble between you and Miss Stokes today?"

"Me and Miss Stokes—hah! Trouble between Ernestus Stokes and the world. Awful old busybody.

Anyway, you should've heard her: 'I'd like to see everyone do his best to keep things shipshape around here.
The other day there were dustballs under the bed, and
now there's a knife in the sink with peanut butter on
it.' Peanut butter, for crying out loud. I mean, I forgot
to wash one lousy knife and—and—I'd like to run it
right through her gizzard. I'd die if I was Miss Tegges
and had her around. I'd positively die."

That last thing I said left me feeling cold all over
and I sat down.

"She's good with Harper, though," said Julie. "Not
at all the way you'd expect—gentle, almost. She gives
her backrubs and makes custard and—"

"Miss Tegges hates custard. We had a deal once: I
was supposed to eat up all the custard and tell Ernestus
Stokes thank-you-very-much. And—and—there she is,
shoving it down Miss Tegges's throat."

"Oh, come on, Slug. She doesn't, you know that.
We all know Harper doesn't have much appetite anymore, but nobody forces anything."

"I still wish we didn't need her and her top-sergeant
ways. I wish we could manage without her."

"No way," said Julie. "We need all the help we can
get. And it's going to be worse, the closer Harper gets
to—"

"No. Don't say it." I jumped up and cracked my
knee against the table. My eyes filled with tears and
the room seemed to swim in front of me. I caught my
breath and rubbed hard on my leg before I hobbled

over to the refrigerator and filled a glass with ice cubes. Lately it seemed that every time I turned around I had tears running down my face, and the really weird thing was that I had never been a crier before. Not when I was little and kids used to try and start something on the playground—they learned better than to tangle with me. Not when Nelson Trimper and his gang set a garbage can on fire in front of Gussie's house. Not even when Gussie died. Now whenever I started with the waterworks routine Julie patted the air and got terribly interested in something else, which was okay with me. I mean, what else *would* she do?

This time she read the ads on the back page of the paper as if she were trying to memorize them, waiting until I had poured my Tab and sat back down before she said, "How was Harper last night?"

"Oh, you know. The way she's been lately—quiet and restless at the same time. Even when she's really quiet and you think she's asleep, you know she's not. A couple of times I went over to the bed and she was lying there with her eyes open. Watching.

"And when it was starting to get light, she began to talk. All about her mother and father and the paint set they brought her from Richmond once. For a time she thought somebody was there, Aunt Something or other, and she got mad. Told her—Aunt Agnes, that was it—what she could do with her mustard plaster and her chamomile tea. It was weird, almost like the other person *was* there. Real, kind of. The way her Mama and Papa and her brothers seem real to me now.

"Richard too, only not as much. And Suzanne. A couple of times during the night she reached out to me and squeezed my hand—well, you could tell she was trying to squeeze it—and said, 'Suzanne?' But I don't know who Suzanne is, do you?"

Julie shook her head slowly. "It's a name she mentions from time to time, then seems to shy away from. But it sounds as if you didn't get any rest at all last night. Why don't you—"

"Well, what did you expect? I mean, did you want me to just curl up and go to sleep? And leave her there all fretful, as Gussie used to say. Criminy, even Ginger had her eyes open."

"You watched with her. Really watched," said Julie, sliding her hand across the table toward me, then pulling it back just as I drew away from her.

"Huh?"

"Oh, nothing. Just that you ought to try to sleep now. Take that fan from the living room and put it in your bedroom. I'm going to the store, so the house will be quiet. Sleep for a couple of hours."

"No. I can't," I said, getting up and moving around the kitchen. I stood at the back door for a minute, looking out and willing myself not to cry. I took a banana off the top of the refrigerator, stared at it, and put it back. "I'm not tired. Besides, I thought I'd go over there later on. Maybe there's something I can do, while Ernestus Stokes keeps everything shipshape."

"Slug, no," said Julie. "I want you to rest. And I want you to do something else. Nothing to do with Harper Tegges. Go for a walk—downtown—to the aquarium. Take a nap and later on we'll go somewhere together."

It was tempting. I mean, here was Julie acting like a mother, and part of me wanted to lean back against her words and let them wrap themselves around me. But something inside told me I had to keep on fighting. "Why?" I said.

"Because I'm afraid you're getting too involved in all this."

"*You're* involved in it, too. It was *your* idea."

"Yes, yes. But I'm *older*. I can be more detached now."

My mouth moved with words I wasn't sure I wanted to say. I watched as Julie opened and closed the cupboards, pausing to add to her grocery list. I started for the door, then swung back as the words came spilling out: "More detached? Than what? I mean, you detached yourself from me and Gussie and Brian. From Monica, too." I hurt with what I had said, but by this time I couldn't seem to stop. "You said—you said before how the worst loss in your life was losing Monica, as if I—me—when I was a baby—didn't matter at all." It took all the concentration I had *not* to cry. I stared past Julie's head at the rose of Sharon tree framed in the kitchen window, at the dark-red flower with the bee cupped inside. It seemed hours before I could look at her, but when I did I saw the muscles working in her throat.

It was hours again before she spoke. "It wasn't like that," she said. "My leaving had nothing to do with you. I didn't even *know* you. I couldn't know you. Because at that time I didn't have enough self to know anyone."

I turned away, and for a minute we stood as if part of a tableau. Then I heard Julie stirring in back of me.

"Can't you try—won't you—" She sighed and went on. "Maybe later, afterward, we can sort things out between us, but right now there's so much going on. With Harper, I mean. It's just that I don't want you to wear yourself out. Okay?"

"Yeah, okay," I said, the fight gone out of me.

"There's a letter for you on the hall table. It's from Brian."

I went to get the letter and came back, opening it and reading it quickly, dropping it on the table as I said, "They love Florence, and they went to Siena and they loved that, too, and want to go back again. You can read it if you want."

"Thanks," said Julie. "Have you written to him yet?"

I thought of all the letters I had started and balled up and thrown into the trash. "No," I said. "Not to Brian. Or to Henley for a while. Or to Dr. Mercy,

either. I mean, what am I going to say—that I'm helping an old woman to die?"

"To live. You're helping her to live well, the time
she's got left."

And it was as if Julie's words reminded me of something I had known and forgotten and knew again. I
looked down at my hands and back at her. "The funny
thing is that I really *like* Miss Tegges now. I like her
toughness, and the way she just always did her own
thing. And even the way she had to be the only one
who mattered. Nobody else. But you can't put all that
in a letter. It sounds so—I don't know—" I waited
until Julie had picked up her list and her pocketbook
and started for the door before I called out, "It does
matter, doesn't it? What we're doing?"

"It matters very much." Julie turned and came back
to the center of the room, leaning against the counter
and picking at the corner of her list. "You know what
I've been thinking? That maybe this is the kind of
nursing I might want to do for a while. I got sort of
burned out by hospital work—the red tape, mountains
of paper, forms, and all. But I knew that being a school
nurse was only an in-between. I just never knew in
between *what*."

The whole time she was speaking, she looked young
and excited, somehow vulnerable, maybe the way she
had looked in New York when she was marching or
protesting or doing whatever it was she did. For a minute I felt as if I were the mother and my mother the

child. "That'd be terrific. *You'd* be terrific. The way you are with Miss Tegges, knowing what to say and do." The words came as a surprise to me, as if I'd said them in spite of myself.

"Do you think so? Really?" said Julie, standing up straight and letting a smile spread across her face.

There was a silence then, as if for a moment we had come too close.

"I'm off to the store," said Julie. "And you—"

"I know," I said. "Take a nap."

"You know what?" I said one morning a few days later, as Julie and I were having breakfast. "At first, well, when I first came here, I mean, there was so much of Harper Tegges. The artist part, and the everyday person, too."

Julie leaned forward, waiting for me to go on.

"But now it's as if her whole world is receding. As if she were cutting off the edges of her life, sort of. Getting smaller and smaller—like something going in on itself. And soon there won't be anything at all. Like she never was."

"No," said Julie, half rising from her chair. "No. It's not like that at all. Maybe now, and for a while, there's a kind of numbness. But look at it this way—you know that Gussie *was*. And my father, your grandfather, even though you never knew him. And Monica. You've got to know that."

"Well, maybe," I said, not quite convinced, getting

up to wash the dishes and putting them in the rack. "I've got to go now. If I'm late, Ernestus Stokes'll eat me alive."

As I went across the street I kicked a stone, stopping from time to time to work it out of the gutter with my toe so I could kick it again, and thought about how I wasn't at all sure that once Miss Tegges was dead I would even remember her being here. And that thought made me shiver. When I got to the bottom of the porch steps I picked up the stone and rubbed it down the side of my shorts, storing it in my pocket as a kind of talisman. I took a deep breath, another, and then another: for Ernestus Stokes, for Miss Tegges, and for me. I went up the steps.

When Miss Stokes answered the door I thought that she seemed somehow defeated. Her hair, fastened back in a bun, had a slightly blowsy look, and her shirttail crept over the waistband of her skirt.

"Things haven't gone well," she said, running her hand over her brow. "The truth is, I'm way behind. I haven't even—"

"Oh, I'm sorry," I said, really beginning to feel sorry for her. But my words seemed to drift off as I found myself looking down at Miss Stokes's feet. I'd've guessed she slept in army boots, I thought, staring at the red quilted slippers with yellow pom-poms that seemed to grow and bobble there like giant dandelions, making her look far less intimidating than usual.

I turned myself around, forcing my eyes onto the window, the walls, the paintings propped on easels. But no matter where I looked I seemed surrounded by dancing pom-poms. I felt a laugh coming on. Oh, Lord, I thought, closing my mouth tight. Don't let me. Help. My thoughts seemed to spin along recklessly. Maybe she wears bikini pants with *Bloomies* across the seat. Black lace bras and— I clenched my hands into fists, wrapping my arms across my chest. By day she's Ernestus Stokes and at night she turns into—

"She slept heavily, and when she woke she was disoriented, and stubborn. No bath. No breakfast. It was all I could do to get her turned. I hoped to have it all done by the time I had to leave. I like things to be in order. Tidied up, you might say." There was a sudden staccato beat to Miss Stokes's words, and when I turned back to her she was tying the laces of her black leather shoes. There was just a glimpse of yellow over the top of her canvas tote bag as she stood up, fastening it securely over her arm.

"I'd stay longer—I'm not one to leave a task undone —but the oil-burner man is coming to clean the furnace between nine and twelve and I have to be there."

"No problem," I assured her. "I'll get Miss Tegges something to eat, and maybe later, when Julie comes, she'll feel more like a bath."

"Very good," said Miss Stokes, moving to the side of the bed. She brushed the backs of her fingers rhythmically against Miss Tegges's cheek, turned abruptly and went out the door. Down on the sidewalk, she stopped, looking back and saying, "She sleeps more and more now, but when she wakes, remember, there's custard in the refrigerator."

I held my hand tight against my mouth and watched as she headed up the hill, briskly at first, then slower, as if the canvas tote bag weighed heavily against her.

"Yellow pom-poms," I said, leaning over the side of the bed. "Ernestus Stokes wears yellow pom-poms." I watched Miss Tegges's face, waiting for her eyebrows to quirk upward.

"And just remember, there's baked custard in the refrigerator." Now she'll say, "Disgusting," I thought. And open her eyes and— A trickle of spit dribbled out of the corner of her mouth; I wiped at it with a Kleenex. Her face was rubbery to touch and I realized that she was still asleep. I stepped back, feeling cross, as if we had been playing catch and Miss Tegges had deliberately missed the ball.

I moved around the room, looking for something to do. Everything there smacked of Ernestus Stokes and wanted undoing. The window shades were neatly drawn and I raised them, letting each one spin and snap satisfyingly against the top of the frame. The magazines were arranged in formation on the coffee table and I toppled them, letting them fall into a comfortable kind of clutter. I went into the kitchen and spread peanut butter on a piece of bread and stood eating it, looking out the window at a cardinal sitting on a tree limb in the Nortons' yard. When I heard Miss Tegges's voice I dropped the bread onto the drainboard and hurried over to her.

"Orange juice. I want orange juice," she said. Her eyes were wide open and she was looking somewhere beyond me. "Come on, John. I don't care what Mama says, or Dr. Lynch, or Aunt Agnes, either. I don't care about the mumps. It won't sting. Won't hurt at all. And I want it. Sneak it up the back steps and—" She curled and uncurled the fingers on her right hand.

"Good morning," I said. "Now that you're awake I'll get you something for breakfast. Orange juice to start. Okay?" Then I went quickly over to the kitchen before she could change her mind.

When I came back, carrying the juice, Miss Tegges had pushed the button to raise the top of her bed. She sat huddled there, her head dangling forward, so that for a minute I thought she was asleep again.

"Here you go," I said, holding the glass with the straw in it toward her. "Now I'll fix you some—"

Her hands seemed to fly out of control, jerking upward, hitting the glass and sending a shower of juice onto her chest. An orange stain spread across the front of her gown and she started to shiver, plucking at it and saying, "Cold . . . cold . . . cold . . . cold."

"Oh, Lord—bathtime, ready or not," I said, running to the bathroom, where I gathered up towels and a washcloth and filled a basin with warm water, all the time wondering whether I could call Julie, knowing that I couldn't even as I thought it. Or that I wouldn't. I came back and lined everything on the tray table, going off again for a clean nightgown and a bath sheet.

"Okay," I said, lowering the bed and reaching behind her neck to untie the strings of the gown. "Let's get that off—it's got to feel cold and clammy." I stopped, waiting for Miss Tegges to take over: to slip out of the gown, reach for the washcloth; to bathe herself while I went off to water the plants or see about breakfast, coming back just in time to take away the dirty water and gather the towels into a bundle for the laundry.

Miss Tegges's arms lay heavily at her sides as she looked up at me, saying, "Cold. Cold." I'm not supposed to do this, I thought. People give themselves baths. Grownups, at least. Even little kids do. And cats. Everybody. Miss Tegges always did before. Or maybe Julie. Or Ernestus Stokes. Not me. Never me. Finally, taking a deep breath, I pulled the gown away from her neck, peeling it down, lifting her arms out one at a time. I tried not to look at her shoulders, at her sunken chest, with her shriveled breasts, the nipples a dark reddish brown. But even when I covered her with a bath sheet, it was as if the outline of her naked body burned through.

As I wiped Miss Tegges's face with the washcloth, I had to work at keeping my own face still, to keep my fingers from pulling back. I've got to *say* something, I thought. I can't just keep doing this and— "It's hot out there today," I said in desperation. "Julie said it's going to be in the nineties. She heard it on the radio."

"Cold," Miss Tegges said.

I dipped the cloth into the water and wrung it out. I pulled back the towel, washing her chest and stomach, under her arms, dabbing at the skin that hung in folds.

"It was so hot I could hear the crickets this morning," I said as I replaced the towel and eased the sheet down, suddenly aware of jagged hipbones, the triangular patch of scraggly gray hair. "Hot-weather bugs, Gussie called them."

Looking somewhere across the room, I thrust the washcloth down between her legs, catching my breath at the sudden sour smell.

When I stopped to wet the cloth again, Miss Tegges struggled up, leaning on one elbow and looking down at herself. She shuddered and pulled her legs up, bending them at the knee as if to make sure they belonged to her.

"Oh, God," she said, dropping back on the bed. "Oh, my God, is that me? Like that?"

Words spun through my head so quickly I couldn't catch them. Slowly, carefully, I eased her onto her side. "You've been very sick," I said out loud. "Maybe you've lost some weight."

"I was an artist's model once. When I first went to New York. The studios—cold—and sometimes the radiators clanged. Did I tell you that? I told someone, somebody. You—Julie—David. His mother sent flowers and I don't know what happened to them. If Mama had known about the modeling. Nude. 'No daughter of mine,' she would say. 'Not my daughter. Not Papa's. John's sister. Never.' Me. Yes. Yes."

I sprinkled powder on Miss Tegges's back and rolled her down flat again.

"Richard said I was beautiful. He liked to look at me—at night. And in the morning. In my bath." She reached out, stroking her stomach, pulling her hand back quickly. "When we were out in Washington— in the house by the field—we had a tub with feet on it and it was big enough for the two of us."

I slid the clean gown over her arms, working it up over her chest.

"It scratches," she said, tugging at the cloth with unexpected strength. "I can't wear this. You said black. Something filmy, with flounces. With beads that jangle and— Rent money be damned. You *lied* to me." Her eyes were wide and angry, and she twisted around as if looking for someone.

When she spoke again she was calm, as though she were answering a question. "When I got my first studio, just after I moved into it, a friend came to stay. While she got back on her feet. Found a job and— She hadn't any money toward the rent so she made me a dress out of black chiffon and I wore it to the Rainbow Room. She was going to be another Hattie Carnegie, another somebody. But she gave up and went back to where she came from. Arkansas. New Jersey. Iowa. It doesn't matter where—only that she went back. I never did. Never."

I moved Miss Tegges onto her side, struggling to change the draw sheet, easing her back while I did the other half. As I went to pull the top sheet up, I saw her holding one leg just above the bed, turning it from side to side, looking at it. And I had to catch myself to keep from tucking the covers quickly around her, from hiding her knobby knees and the feet that seemed suddenly too big for her legs.

Sitting on the side of the bed, I poked at the pillows behind her head. "Boy, I'm not much at this bath business, am I? And a bed is always lumpier after I make it than it was before. That was one thing about Gussie. I mean, she didn't *care* about things like that."

"Do you think I'm ugly?" Miss Tegges caught me by the arm, pulling herself up so that she was swaying forward. "*Do you think I'm ugly?*"

And without thinking about it I threw my arms around her, hugging her close, unbalancing her so that she fell against me, her bald head hooked over my shoulder.

"Harper Tegges, I think you're one terrific person." And I felt her hands, the fingers sharp and bony, making patting motions on my back.

The bus stopped, and started, and stopped again. It belched fumes that were caught up and carried along, forcing their way in through the open windows and making me feel half sick.

"Well now," said Julie, fanning at the air in front of her face. "That was nice. A good lunch and a day out. It's good to get away. Do something different."

All that forced cheeriness settled over me like an attack of claustrophobia. Why does she think she has to keep distracting me, I thought, rubbing the palms of my hands down my skirt. Why can't she let me alone to think the things I want to think? About Miss Tegges, and all the rest of us. What's going to happen and— Even after all these weeks we still can't be quiet together. It got so the more the bus ground along, the more I knew I had to get off, and when it stopped for the light at Thirty-first Street I jumped up, saying, "Since you have to get back to take care of Miss Tegges, I think I'll just get off here and go to the museum. I'll see you back at the house later on." And I was out the middle door and across the street, not turning until I heard the bus pull away from the curb.

Just in time, I thought, sighing and feeling my shoulders start to unknot. Another minute and I would've exploded. I stood looking up at the museum, feeling small and very much in awe. I mean, there wasn't a building in Gussie's whole town that was this big, or this white, or this cool-looking. Even all of Main Street rolled into one, with the bank on top, wouldn't have been this grand. I walked over to one of the gran-

ite lions, staring into his open mouth, his teeth pointing down at me. Gathering my resolve, and in spite of
the heat, I started up the steps, running in diagonals,
like a sailboat tacking into the wnd.

Once inside the door I stopped, amazed by the sense
of space. I moved straight ahead, past the rows of
columns, and the galleries opening on either side, out
the main hall, and into the corridor that enclosed a
courtyard, making a complete circuit back to where I
had begun. I stood, my fingers lightly touching the
glass, and watched the steel lines of a sculpture moving
in the sunlight, then turned to study the mosaics on
the walls. From the moment I had stepped in the front
door I had felt peculiarly at home, as if the museum
and I had accepted each other. I'm not sure, but maybe
it was because of the hours I'd spent in Miss Tegges's
studio with the easels, the smell of paint, and the
brushes sticking, bristle end up, out of jars.

The sign over the door said OLD MASTER PAINTING,
and I found I was walking on tiptoe, listening to the
polished wooden floors crackling beneath my step. I
came forward to read the signs: *Madonna and Child.*
Madonna and Child in a Landscape. Madonna and
Child Enthroned. Criminy, I thought. What's with
this mother-and-child bit? Didn't any of these Old
Master types ever paint apples or sunsets or cabbage
leaves?

I moved into another room, past a guard standing
as if he were stuffed, stopping in front of a picture of a

mother playing with a baby while another woman looked on and a cat slept under a chair. *Motherhood*, the card said, and something pinched inside me. She looks so happy, as if she would never leave, I thought. I went quickly on, past *Family Group* and *Rest on the Flight*, where a mother soothed her child during a journey. But Julie made her flight alone, not on a donkey but on a Trailways bus, I thought, hurrying back out into the corridor and on to another wing.

The paintings here seemed brighter and less ponderous, and I relaxed a bit. I turned into the gallery on the left and stopped, catching my breath at Picasso's *Mother and Child*. I could almost feel the woman's arms tight around the child. Around me.

As I started down the long wall it was as if certain paintings jumped out at me, snagging me, forcing me to stop.

In *In the Garden* by Mary Cassatt I saw a mother holding a child, surrounded by so many flowers I could almost smell them. I moved on to another painting by the same artist, *A Kiss for Baby Anne*. Was I ever fat like that, I wondered as I watched Baby Anne being kissed by a mother who looked strong and gentle and sure to always be there.

I ducked around the corner and came face to face with three people sitting on a bus. *In the Omnibus*. Mary Cassatt, I read, standing back to study them in spite of myself. Grandmother. Mother. Child. Gussie. Julie. Me. No, I thought. No. Never. And I started to run, jostling a woman carrying a campstool, out into the corridor, past the mosaics, and back to the Main Hall. I turned into a gallery with silver displayed in glass cases, walking without seeing, until the pounding in my head stopped. Making my way toward the door, I had my hand up, ready to push it open. Miss Tegges, I remembered. I came for Miss Tegges. I stepped away from the door, leaning against one of the stone columns and feeling the cold through the back of my shirt. And as if I'd known all along where to go, I went into the gallery on the right.

The room was large, with windows rimmed around the ceiling. The walls and carpet were a pale cool gray. I settled onto a bench, letting myself relax before I began, very slowly, to look around.

I knew Miss Tegges's paintings without getting up to read the signs. Knew them the way I would have known familiar faces in a crowd. There were two of them, each on a short corner wall on the east side of the gallery. The colors were vivid, and the spaces and shapes said something to me, so that soon it was as if all the mothers and children in all the other galleries had crouched back and were hiding somewhere in the shadows, away from me.

One Thursday afternoon I was wandering around the house looking for something to do. Not that I usually have to *look* for something to do, but it was one of those funny little folds in time that somehow just seem extra. I mean, Julie was out, I had finished vacuuming the first floor, and I was due over at Miss Tegges's in twenty minutes. I had a new book to start but not enough time to really get into it. In the kitchen I checked the schedule to see who was on duty ahead of me and when I saw it was David I began trying to figure just how early I could get there and still look casual. Ever since David and I had been out a couple of times, it had become somewhat awkward—more so than just running into him outside, or stepping over his feet sticking out from under his car. And I wasn't even sure if the times we'd been out had counted as dates.

The first one was the time he dragged me off, over to Sloane's garage to see what he called his *trompe l'oeil*. The time I wanted to clobber him for asking *Julie* if *I* could go. When we got to the garage, to David's studio, really, I was amazed at how spare it was. Spartan almost. I asked him about that and he said that he couldn't help having the feeling that it wasn't really his, that old man Sloane might repossess it at any minute.

"Is your room at home like this?" I asked, thinking of the clutter that was so much a part of Gussie's house. He stopped for a minute, as if he had to think about it, then said, "Yeah, pretty much, I guess."

"Didn't you ever collect anything?"

"Beer cans," he said. "My father started it, and they just grew and grew. In fact, most guys I know have to argue to keep their mothers from throwing away their collections of bottle caps, license plates, or baseball cards. But not me. I've been trying to get rid of those beer cans for years. Finally one day I just packed them into a leaf bag and hauled them down the cellar. You'd've thought that would've been the end of it, right? Talk about breaking my mother's heart. She got them all out and lined them around the ledge up near the ceiling of the club room, so no matter where you walk you're in danger of being crowned by a Harp Lager or a Truman Brown Ale."

"Why does it matter—to her, I mean?" I asked.

"It doesn't," said David. "But I think she thought my father would flip out. You know something—if he came home with petrified dog turds, I think she'd put them on a shelf in the window."

Then David pointed to his *trompe l'oeil* on the wall opposite the window and said, "There it is—*Feet on Canvas*." And he was right. That was exactly what it looked like. After that there was a long funny pause while I tried to decide whether it would be better to ask to see some of his other work or not; whether he would think I was interested or just nosy. Anyway, I didn't know what to expect and was horribly afraid they were going to be imitations of Miss Tegges's work.

After what seemed like ages I got up my nerve and asked, and for a minute David's face looked as if he couldn't decide whether to say yes or no. Finally he took out one painting and put it up on the easel, and when he stood back I liked what I saw there. I don't really know what to call things in art, but I only know that it was birds and water and sky, but not exactly. Maybe as if he were seeing it through a prism or something. It struck me funny all of a sudden that in grade school art had been my very worst subject. I mean, in first grade when we made clay outlines of our hands, mine looked like I had a mitten on, and Gussie used it as a spoon rest on the stove. And years later, when we got to papier-mâché, my animal didn't look like anybody else's. "Lumpish," Mrs. Prather said when she came to get us from art class that day. But on the last day of school that year, when I had it sitting on my desk to take home, Miss Albright, who was our teacher by then, said it showed a spirited imagination. I guess that says something about the difference between Mrs. Prather and Miss Albright. Anyway, I kept it on the windowsill in my room, until one time it got rained on and sort of settled into a sodden blob.

But I knew, just by looking at David's painting, that I liked it. I knew it was good, too. However I responded must have been the right way, because he showed me another and another and another one after that. Later we went across the street and had pizza before he took me home and hurried back to the garage to work.

One day the following week I was coming out of Miss Tegges's house just as David was getting out of his car with that funny combination of splotches he sometimes has: oil paint and axle grease, as if he'd gone from one to the other. Which he usually has. He asked me if I wanted to go to a movie and I said when. He said in as much time as it took for him to shower, and I said I'd meet him outside. Then I ran for the shower myself, scrubbing away the smells of my hours with Miss Tegges: medicine, disinfectant, and that funny stale smell of sickness that seems to cling to her no matter how often she's bathed and powdered. I hurried, but David must have hurried more, because he was waiting for me, leaning up against his car, when I got outside, my hair hanging loose and wet down my back.

When we got to the movies the 7:30 show was sold out, but we got tickets for the next show and just sort of wandered around. I was hungry, but when David asked me if I was, I said no, because I wasn't sure how he'd feel about my paying my own way. We went into the deli, and when I said I still wasn't hungry, said it loudly to drown out the growling of my stomach, he got himself a corned beef on rye and gave me half. After we finished I went back and got another one—and gave him half.

We went into the library and I got the third in the Barsetshire series, and at the last minute went back and grabbed the fourth, because I always feel like there might be a major disaster and I won't be able to get to the library and there I'll be with nothing to read. David got Gauguin's *The Writings of a Savage* and a book of the artist's work as well—he said he wouldn't feel right borrowing Miss Tegges's books anymore when he couldn't be sure she'd really know that she was lending them. For a minute neither of us said anything. We went downstairs to the children's room, looking at the posters on the walls, pulling our all-time favorite picture books off the shelves. David was really into *Where the Wild Things Are*. He told me how he always thought of himself as Max and how one time when he got the book out of the library for about the twentieth time his father asked him why he didn't read comic books instead. I was always a Babar fan myself, maybe because the old woman sort of reminded me of Gussie. Anyway, by then it was time for the library to close and we had to run for the movies and almost didn't get into the 9:30 show. We also discovered that we both like hot buttered popcorn—with extra butter.

But that was a week ago and I haven't heard from him since.

David and I hardly had a chance to say more than hello, because as soon as I got across the street Miss Tegges called and we had to go to her. She was sitting in her chair in front of the television, her fingers drumming on the tray so that they seemed to play in counterpoint to the voices coming from the set. She looked at me expectantly, and then, as if she didn't know me, let her head drop forward, rocking it slightly to one side and back again.

As David lifted her back into bed, she resisted, arching her back and fighting against him. She jerked her legs outward, kicking into space, and flailed her arms so that I had to catch them and hold them until she was settled against the pillows.

"Turn it off," she said, looking at the television.

"Okay," I said, waving to David as he went out the door. Remembering how Julie said she had tried to get Miss Tegges to watch the ball game, I said, half teasing, "But there's a baseball game tonight, maybe you and Julie can watch it."

"Ball game," she said. "Ball game."

I reached for the switch, and as I watched the picture fade I heard the sound of David starting his lawn mower coming through the open windows and, from somewhere far away, the barking of a dog. Ginger sat up, pricked her ears, and went to the door, scratching to go out.

"I'll be right back," I said, pulling up the side of the bed. "I'm just going to take the dog out for a minute."

After I took Ginger for a quick trip to the woods at the foot of the street, I brought her back, tugging at the leash to get her up the steps and into the house. "After a while we'll go for a long walk, okay? After Julie comes."

As soon as I stepped back into the house I could sense a change in Miss Tegges. I watched her rock her head from side to side, as if trying to clear it of something. Her legs moved restlessly under the covers, and her hands lay, tightened into fists, on her chest.

I went to her, putting one of my hands on top of hers. "What is it? Is something wrong?"

She was suddenly still. Moving slowly, she turned her head, peering out at me as if from far away.

"You came," she said.

"I told you I'd be right back. That I was just taking Ginger out."

"You came. I said you would—no matter what. And they didn't believe me. Julie, and the girl Slug. Mattie-Miller and the rest. And now that you're here—Suzanne."

"No," I said, the word coming quickly in spite of myself. I tried to pull away, but she held me firmly, clenching my hand until I thought my bones would break.

"I'm Slug. Slug October. You know me. Julie Wilgus's daughter from across the street."

"Suzanne," Miss Tegges said, glaring at me fiercely, then changing abruptly to a gentle singsong. "Daughter. Daugh-ter. Daugh-ter."

I sat down on the side of the bed, moving close to her to lessen the tension on my arm. "It's all right now. Everything's all right."

"It's all right now," Miss Tegges repeated after me, and I watched as tears ran down her face.

"I told Richard never to tell you, but he did. I'm glad he did—" she said.

There was a long pause during which everything in the room seemed to stand out: dust motes hanging in sunlight, the sound of the lawn mower as David mowed between the houses, and the hairs that bristled on Ginger's tail. Carefully I tried to ease my hand away from Miss Tegges's grasp, rubbing at my wrist to get rid of the numbness. Her hand darted out, catching at the bedclothes. "Don't go—don't—"

"I'm here. It's all right."

"Suzanne—" she said. "I want to tell you—want you to understand." She pushed herself up, away from the pillows, saying, "It was when I was in California that I met Richard—'A rose is a rose is a'—a friend of a friend of a friend. He was my friend. My best friend, and for a while it was—and we moved to Washington —on Puget Sound and one day I danced on the lawn —across the field. Because of the baby."

I sat ready to catch her if she lurched forward, not sure whether to speak or not to speak.

"It's all right now," Miss Tegges said, leaning back against the pillows. "You don't have to do anything. They take care of me here. You're here, though. Here. Here.

"It had always been the painting—that was all there could ever be." Again she rolled her head fretfully from side to side.

"That was all there could ever be. And when I was forty, forty-one, I'm not sure— There was Richard. And the baby. You. Suzanne." She crossed her arms and rocked them in front of her. "Baby . . . baby . . . baby . . ."

She stopped rocking and hit her hands against her chest, clawing at her breasts through the nightgown. "Pretty baby sucked and sucked—and I was—soon there wouldn't be any more—I knew that I was being all used up. The paintings and the things I had to do.

"I loved the baby. I loved Richard. But there was something I loved more. Had to love more. You have to understand that. Tell me you understand. I've been waiting—have to hear."

"What happened to the baby?" I said, not wanting to ask but asking anyway. "What happened to Suzanne?"

" 'Monday's child is fair of face, Tuesday's child is—' " You were a Tuesday's child. You were full of grace. Pretty baby. I stayed for a year and we played pat-a-cake and blew at dandelions and lay on our backs watching clouds, and all the time I was shattering like glass." Harper's breath was coming quickly, in little gasps. "I told Richard—it was better that way. 'Ladybug, ladybug, fly away'—not home. Never again."

"What did you do?" I felt myself inching backward along the bed. "What did you do?"

"Richard told you. I told him not to, but he must have told. And now you're here. Pretty baby."

"You tell me," I said. "Tell me what you did with Suzanne."

"I left you. Left you with your father, because there wasn't any other way I could stay all in one piece.

There wasn't anything else I could do. You have to understand that. Baby-baby. Baby-baby."

"No. No. I don't understand. I'll never understand," I heard myself screaming as I turned and ran out of the door and down the steps. Away from Miss Tegges's house.

Harper

GOOD BABY—good hand. Good hand. Good hand.

I traded my baby for— No, not that. I took all of me —all that was left—and went away. I told Richard and then I left. Mama's grandchild and she never knew.

I couldn't not go. And I would go again. And oh, my God, it hurt. It hurts.

Richard sent fat envelopes with pictures in them. Suzanne at two and three and four—candles and party hats. Suzanne on a pony, a sliding board, a merry-go-round. Mother. Father. Child. A new mother. Then I didn't look anymore. The mailman brought the envelopes and I put them in the bottom drawer. Didn't open them.

I need something—somebody—

I rang the bell. Julie Wilgus put it there in case I ever— And I rang it, and for a minute there were bells all around me. Clanging back and forth. That was something I always wanted to do.

"What was that?" somebody said.

"Ring the bell."

"You just did," he said. Who said? I wasn't sure.

"Not *that* bell," I said. Not that bell at all. In the Episcopal church at home—on the other side of the street and down a block. It was there, with a big, thick, bristly rope that hung down from the belfry, and every Sunday we had to walk right past it to get into the services. Mama and Papa. Edwin. Francis. With John and me bringing up the rear. Reaching out to touch it. Knowing that someday we would come back—just the two of us, on a weekday, of course—and ring that bell to beat the band. Tugging on the rope, swinging on it so that our feet barely skimmed the floor. We were going to, but we never did. Bell's gone. Gone.

"Here it is," the somebody said, as if I had spoken out loud. It was David from next door, I think, climbing up from the floor with a small brass bell in his hand. It made a dull clicking sound and wasn't the right bell at all.

"I told you not that bell. I rang it and nobody came. Julie Wilgus said they would and they didn't. There was no one here."

"I'm here," David said.

"And I'm here now, too," said Julie, from somewhere in back of him.

"She's gone. Suzanne was here and I told her—tried to tell her. And now she's gone."

Slug

I WENT up to the corner and got a bus, not sure where I was going until I got to the library. It wasn't until I sort of woke up in the middle of the fiction section that things began to register. I was leaning against the S's; once I even took out a copy of John Steinbeck's *Tortilla Flat* and looked at it before putting it back. After that I just sat there, looking around me, watching a woman balancing a baby on her hip while she swung the paperback rack round and round, and an old man as he tried to explain to the librarian that he needed a book for his wife, who had the flu, but he wasn't at all sure what she had already read. When a girl came along with a cart of books, reaching for shelves just over my head, I slid out of the way, but as soon as she left I moved back again—almost as if John Steinbeck and I were keeping company.

After a while I went downstairs, settling on the floor in the far corner of the room, pulling several picture books off the shelf and spreading them out around me, as if I were building a moat. I don't know how long it was after that that David came along and sat cross-legged on the floor beside me, picking up *The Little House* and flipping the pages.

"Are you reading these or—"

"No," I said, knowing distantly that I wasn't surprised to see him. "I just figured if I put them there somebody would think I was doing something. Librarians are all for people *doing* things."

"There isn't one," said David.

"One what?"

"Librarian."

"Oh," I said, looking up and rubbing my eyes. "There was. She must have gone someplace. To lunch or—"

"More likely supper," he said, turning the last page before he put the book down. "What I mean is, it's late. It's been a long time."

I turned away from him, sliding a large green book back and forth until the rasping sound it made against the floor seemed to rise up and fill the room.

"Look, I know it's none of my business," said David, "but if there's anything I can do—"

"There's nothing."

"Come on, Slug. It's tough on all of us, going in there with Miss Tegges like that. Watching her get worse until— As far as I'm concerned there'd be something *wrong* if it didn't get you down from time to time."

"It doesn't," I said.

"But something—"

"You were right the first time."

"What?"

"It's none of your business."

David stopped for a minute and then went on as if I hadn't spoken. "All I can say is that something has to have set you off, to send you flying out of there and up the hill. To leave Harper in the house alone, as sick as she is. I mean, I could understand your all of a sudden panicking at the whole thing, but you said it wasn't that, so—"

"So what? All you care about is your precious Harper Tegges."

"I thought that was the point. To care about her. Not run the hell off."

"I had to."

"Why?"

"Because."

"Because why?" said David. By now we were talking in hard-edged whispers.

I jumped up, gathering the books and stuffing them back into their cubbyholes. "You don't know what she did."

"But what *could* she do? Drool? Wet the bed? Or think maybe her Aunt Agnes had come for another visit?"

I moved to the other side of the room and stood in front of the globe of the world, spinning it and letting my fingers trail across oceans and continents. "She left Suzanne," I said.

"Who?" David moved closer so he could hear me.

"Suzanne. Her daughter. Her baby daughter."

And before he could say anything I went on, the words spilling out of me, the globe spinning faster and faster beneath my fingers. "I mean, there she is—Miss Tegges—always so, oh, I don't know. Independent. And I thought she was so great. Doing things her own way. Not bothering *with* anybody. Not *bothering* anybody else. Except all the time there was this kid, this baby named Suzanne. And she left her. Don't you understand? She left her the way Julie left me."

I let go of the globe and stood leaning on the frame, my head down, my shoulders shaking.

"Slug, don't," said David, pulling at my arm. I turned and fell against him, and he held me close, rocking me back and forth, until the shaking stopped. Still holding me by the shoulders, he moved back, looking down at me.

"Don't. Don't take your anger at Julie out on Miss Tegges. It's—"

And I was away from him, catching my breath and saying, "I'm not. That's not it at all. You don't know anything about it—about me or Julie, either."

The librarian came down the steps and into the room, carrying an armload of books, tumbling them onto the nearest table. She looked from me to David to the pile of books, and moved over to her desk, sitting down and opening and closing drawers as if to say she was there and she wasn't going to leave.

"Come on. Let's get out of here. Go somewhere we can talk," he said, nodding in the direction of the stairs.

I ran past him and up the steps. I hurried through the library to the outside and stood looking up and down the street, trying to decide what to do.

"Look," said David, coming through the door a few steps behind me. "Let's go get something to eat. Okay?"

I still didn't say anything, but when he opened the car door I got in and sat staring straight ahead.

"Look at that old guy over there in the corner, the one taking the newspaper apart," said David when we were settled at a table in the back of the deli. "What do you think his story is?"

I thought for a minute while I pushed the sauerkraut back inside my Reuben. "He bought a lottery ticket, and he's looking to see if he won."

"And if he did?" said David.

"He'll buy a racehorse . . ."

"And he'll—the racehorse'll win the Kentucky Derby and after that . . ."

By this time we were both leaning forward, straining to see which part of the paper the man was reading.

"Forget it," David said as we watched him fold the

entertainment section of the paper and get up. "He's going to the movies."

"How about that woman over there," I said. And we were off again, spinning stories about the people around us. Staying deliberately away from the things I wasn't ready to talk about.

When we finished eating David got up and went to the bakery counter, coming back with a white paper bag. "Here, I got cookies. Want a cup of coffee?"

But the deli seemed to be closing in around me the way the library had, and Miss Tegges's house before that. "No," I said, getting up and bunching the trash together, pushing the straw wrapper down inside my paper cup. "Let's get out of here. I'll make some coffee at home and we can drink it out back. Julie's at Miss Tegges's anyway. Okay?"

"Maybe I shouldn't have said what I did, about your taking your anger at Julie out on Miss Tegges," said David when we were settled on Julie's back steps with mugs of coffee.

"But?" I said.

"But what?"

"A 'maybe' is usually followed by a 'but,' " I said. "Like dropping the other shoe."

"Okay then, *but*—I don't think one has to do with the other. Miss Tegges isn't Julie. *You're* not Suzanne. I mean, I don't know much about you and Julie, only what you've said—that this is your first time together."

"You mean that blatherskite mailman didn't tell, clumping up and down the street toting gossip and ads from Radio Shack? All about how Julie Wilgus had this baby and she left it in a red coaster wagon and went ahead and got on the first Trailways bus that came along."

"Even *our* mailman wouldn't know all that. Where'd you get blatherskite, anyway?"

"It was Gussie's word. What she said about the people in town who wondered about the things Gussie didn't want to talk about. Like where Julie went and was she coming back and who the father of her baby was. Me. *My* father. Do you know something—Julie doesn't even know. She told me that herself." After I had said that, I couldn't look at him.

David put his arm around my shoulder, and after a while, with his left hand, he reached in the bag and handed me a cookie.

But I pulled away from him and it bounced down the steps and onto the ground. "I thought Miss Tegges was different," I said. "Not like everybody else."

"Not like Julie, you mean," said David.

"Not like Julie, then." I banged my mug down on the step. "And another thing—the other day I went to the art museum and all the pictures there were nothing but mothers and children, and it was as if they were all reaching off the walls at me—"

"All?" David had a look on his face that could have been the beginning of a laugh.

"Some, then," I said, thinking that the things I was saying weren't coming out quite the way I wanted them to. I went on, anyway. "And the books Miss Tegges has. I looked at them one day when she was asleep. Mary Cassatt. Berthe Morisot. Mothers and kids everywhere. Playing hide-and-seek, catching butterflies. On the balcony. In the garden. By the sea. Like it's the way things should be."

"Not exactly a scientific experiment," David said.

"Don't get scientific with me. And don't lecture. Besides, I never had Julie. And Suzanne didn't have her mother, either." David cleared his throat as if he was going to say something but didn't. I mean, what was there *to* say?

"Let's talk about something else," I said after a while. And we did: about teachers and summer vacations and our all-time favorite Christmas presents. David told me about the first time he knew that painting was all he ever wanted to do and about the picture he had sold from the show at school last year and how every once in a while he wondered about the person who bought it. We listened to Ernestus Stokes closing her first-floor windows and saw the lights go out in the houses on the next street over and watched the hollyhocks along the back fence making shadows in the moonlight.

And I thought about Miss Tegges again.

Once, years ago, I had a toothache and Gussie had doctored it with oil of cloves, and afterward for minutes on end my tooth would stop hurting and I could almost sleep. Until wham—the pain was back again. That's the way it was now. With Miss Tegges and what she had done. With Julie.

The pain was back.

"It's still not all right," I said the way I had said, "It still hurts," to Gussie about my tooth. "It's never going to be all right." We sat for a while listening to the rustling of the wind in the poplar trees until I said, "Do you know what Miss Tegges said? That Suzanne sucked the life away. Her life—her artist's life."

"That's the way it was for her. The only way it could be for her. That's not to say it was right or wrong but—"

"It was wrong," I said. "It was wrong."

"But it's over. It's the past, Slug. Let it be."

David got up and walked to the end of the yard, coming back to stand just in front of me. "It's not going to be much longer, is it?" he said. "With Miss Tegges, I mean."

I felt cold all over.

"I asked your m—asked Julie, and she said it could go fast from here on."

"When I was at the museum I saw her paintings," I said, remembering the way I knew Miss Tegges had painted them without even reading the cards.

"That's what makes me so sick about what's happening to her. That they *are* so good." David turned suddenly and moved down to the fence again.

And I was up and after him, standing beside him, plucking leaves off the hollyhocks and shredding them, dropping the pieces onto the ground. "You make me so mad—you— Miss Tegges is going to die and it's as if all you care about are the paintings. As if that's all she's good for. How about *her*—the way she was. Even the way she is. As a person, I mean."

My words seemed to hang there between us. Me defending Miss Tegges. And the funny thing was, I meant what I was saying, just like I meant what I had said a few minutes before. None of it made sense, and I swung away from David, but he came after me, catching at my hand and holding it until my fingers ached.

"I've got to go," he said. "I have to be at the garage at seven." But instead of moving he stood where he was, saying finally, "It wasn't only that—about Harper, I mean."

"I know," I said. "I know."

And then we were together, holding on to each other and swaying there, never wanting to let go.

After a while David stepped back and looked at me. "We could go inside," he said. "And watch Johnny Carson."

"We could," I said. "Only I thought you had to get home."

"I've changed my mind."

When David finally left I walked out onto the front porch with him. He started across the street, stopped, and called back to me, "Will you go to see Miss Tegges tomorrow?"

I turned toward the door, pretending I didn't hear him. Because about tomorrow—I just didn't know.

Harper

THEY'RE LAYERED there, like paint on canvas. One after the other, so that at times it's hard to tell—to make them out. A kind of pentimento.

Mama and Papa, Aunt Agnes, old Dr. Lynch. My brothers Edwin and Francis, and John, who was the closest—we were almost like twins. Suzanne, Slug, and Julie Wilgus. Mattie-Miller, Ernestus Stokes, David, and the people from the hospital. Richard didn't come. He couldn't—after what— But it had to be.

It's done. The work—the paintings. Brushes—canvases—the way the pencil feels against my hand. That was all there was—all there could ever be, but it was enough. Had to be enough.

And I have to let it go. I know that now. But not yet. Not quite yet.

Julie

"How DARE you do that. How dare you go off and leave her there. What'd you think, that Ginger the dog was going to take your shift?" I stood at the screen door saying the things I wanted to say to Slug just under my breath and waiting for someone to come and take my place with Harper so I could go home and really give her a piece of my mind. "Irresponsible," I said, knowing that I was sounding like a mother and somehow unable to do anything about it.

I saw Mattie-Miller coming down the street, a bundle of magazines stuffed under one arm, a knitting bag trailing strands of wool in the other. Just as she turned onto the walk, one of her dogs shot out of the underbrush, cutting across the yard, planting his muddy paws on her shoulders and sending the magazines slipping and sliding to the ground. By the time I got outside, she had gathered them up and come huffing up on the porch.

"What a greeting," she said, dropping her things onto a chair and dabbing at her face with a flowered handkerchief. She jutted out her lower lip and blew so that her hair bounced against her forehead. "It is hot, indeed it is," she said, pulling a cloud of pink-and-lavender wool out of the bag and holding it up for me to see. "I always like to bring lots of things to do. Projects, you might call them. Like this afghan." And Mattie-Miller swirled the wool around her like a bullfighter's cloak. "My church has a bazaar just before Christmas and I like to do my part. So far I've made a pink and green, a yellow and green, and now this one —almost done. But next year," she said, rolling the afghan and stuffing it back into the bag, "next year I've already told them I'm doing antimacassars, dresser scarves, placemats. It's too hot for all this." She reached for her handkerchief again.

"It's lovely," I said, inching my way toward the steps and thinking that sleeping under that froth of pink and purple would be a real psychedelic experience. "I have to run now. There's something I have to take care of at home."

"But tell me how Miss Tegges was last night," she said, following me down the steps. "Is there anything I should know about?"

"Just that there's a new bottle of her seizure medicine on top of the refrigerator. She was quiet, slept pretty well." I moved away from her and was poised, as if on first base and ready to steal second, when she grabbed for me, catching me under the elbow and leading me back toward the porch.

"Wait, there's something I have to show you. Something I brought for Miss Tegges." She rummaged in her knitting bag and pulled out another paperweight, shaking it to set the snowstorm in motion before she handed it to me. "I had gotten her one before, put it right beside her bed, and I can't for the life of me figure out what happened to it." Just then we heard the sound of Harper's bell, and Mattie-Miller turned, gathering up her belongings as she went, and hurried inside, while I, without thinking about it, shoved the paperweight down in my pocket and ran across the street.

When I got home the front door was locked and I went around back, fishing down the side of the window box for the spare key and opening the door, ready to say the things I had been thinking all night.

I knew the house was empty as soon as I stepped inside.

Emptier than it had been in all the years I had lived alone. I went through the kitchen, stopping to put my hand on the kettle to see if Slug had had her morning cup of tea. It was cold, and there were no dishes in the sink. The downstairs had the kind of order that usually takes hold of a place when the people who live in it are away, and I moved to open the living-room windows, throwing them up as high as they would go. The chill in the house seemed to be of long standing, though I had seen lights on last night; had watched Slug and

David come in, and David leave later on. I had seen the light burning in Slug's room long into the night, every time I had gone to check on Harper. Busybody, I said to myself, and cringed at the thought of Slug knowing I had been spying on her. Not spying. Looking out for. Wondering about. "Well, what does she expect," I said out loud. "Running off like that. Leaving Harper alone yesterday and—"

Running off. And I was up the steps, pushing at the walls of the stairwell, my mind working faster than my legs.

She's gone. Gathered up her stuff sometime during the night and taken off. Without a word—a by-your-leave.

So that we didn't even last the year.

It was a dumb idea, the thought that we could go back. Start again. And yesterday, at Harper's, what must have happened. Like adhesive ripped against a cut. If that's the way she wants it, then—

I pushed open the door of Slug's room and went inside and stood looking around. The bed was unmade, with the T-shirt she slept in lying on the floor next to a pair of jeans. The drawers were hanging open and I was surprised to see clothes inside—the last time I noticed, she had been living out of that old tattered suitcase she brought with her. I looked around for it and found it partway under the bed and, nudging it open with my foot, stared down at a tangle of sweaters and socks. There were books piled on the bedside table, an empty Tab bottle, and a funny old windup alarm clock, whose ticking seemed to get louder and louder, and without thinking I picked it up and stuffed it under the pillow. I moved over to the dresser, looking at a pair of hoop earrings, a roll of stamps, and a picture of Slug and Henley in a plastic frame. There was a yellow powder puff dropped, fuzzy side up, just on the edge of the bureau. I started to move forward, stopped, and caught my breath, looking down at the floor, where two of Slug's footprints stood out darkly in the center of a dusting of talcum powder.

It was almost as if she were standing there, and I sat down on the side of the bed before looking again. This time the footprints seemed to mock me, as if Slug had paused just briefly before going on. If she's gone I don't care, I told myself. So far this summer we haven't gotten anywhere at all, just chipping away at the year stretching out ahead of us until Brian comes back and Slug can go with him. It'll be better that way. Now I can stop trying, can put my life back the way it was and go on from there.

I looked around again and thought that the room looked more empty than abandoned. Not the way I would have left it, anyway. Not the way I had left another room in another house.

It had come to me after lunch that I was going to leave. I had been washing the dishes, the mismatched plates and cups with whiskery cracks on the insides, while behind me Gussie upended her shopping bag onto the table. Out of the corner of my eye I saw a glass doorknob start to roll and saw my mother dive for it. The baby cried and I took a bottle out of the refrigerator, put it on the stove in a pan of water, and when it was ready I went to Slug, picked her up, and took her out onto the front porch. For once I wasn't impatient for her to finish but sat on Gussie's old metal glider, rocking her back and forth as if I had all the time in the world, watching the soft spot on the top of her head pulse in and out beneath her fuzz of dark hair, knowing, in a removed sort of way, that the next time she had to be fed I wouldn't be there.

When she had finished I put her back in the basket under the front-room window and went upstairs to my own room, closing the door behind me. And I put it in order, because by that very order I was saying that I was never coming back. I gathered up the movie magazines, the draggled balloons with the air seeped out, the plastic jewelry box with the dancing ballerina who no longer danced on top, and the pictures of the boys' basketball team and carried them down to the trash, going out the front door and around to the side of the house. I remember wondering if Gussie would find the treasures in her own garbage cans. I went back upstairs and made the bed, pulling the covers tight and flat. I straightened the clothes in the bureau drawers, the ones I was leaving behind, and lined the shoes—a pair of sandals and a pair of pink tennis shoes with polka-dot laces—along the back wall of the closet. There was a box with money in it under the bed and I pulled it out, knowing at last what I had been saving it for, emptying it into my pocketbook. When I went downstairs, shoving my little suitcase out onto the porch, and told Gussie that I was going downtown for diaper pins, she didn't look up from the baubles spread out on the table in front of her. "Baby's crying," she said, as if I didn't *hear* the baby crying. So I took up Slug and said that I would take her with me, give her a little outing in my mother's red coaster wagon.

I stood up, looking around Slug's room again and thinking that I didn't *know* how she would leave it if she wasn't coming back. That I didn't really know her at all.

She went to the library, I thought. And realizing that the library didn't open until noon, I cast about for something else. To the store, the post office. For a walk. But she has to be at Harper's at one, to take over from Mattie-Miller, I said, telling myself what I knew I knew, then immediately doubting it. I ran downstairs and checked the schedule on the bulletin board: Slug 1–5.

Back upstairs I stood in the doorway of the room for a minute, before I moved cautiously inside, determined now to see if anything was missing. I reached for the top drawer to look for her wallet, but it was as if something were pulling me back, telling me that I had no right. No business. I turned and went downstairs and out onto the porch.

I had been sitting in the same place on the porch yesterday when I saw Slug run out of Harper Tegges's house and up the hill. But I saw it with a kind of detachment and a delayed sense of reaction. After all, I've never been much used to watching for other people. Just as I've never had much to do with waiting for people to come home, with curfews, report cards, and teacher conferences. I saw David stop pushing the lawn mower and go inside, and after what seemed like ages my brain started to work. Why David and why not Slug? Did he need any help, and what about Harper?

When I got over there, David was just crawling out from under the bed with the bell I had given Harper in his hand. But Harper didn't want any part of it, talking on and on instead about the services in the Episcopal church and the bell she and her brother John were always going to ring but never had. She was restless, tossing back and forth on the bed, but strangely elated at the same time, so that I had to work at hearing what David was saying. He had seen Slug go up the street and not paid much attention, thinking only that someone had come to relieve her, until he thought he heard Harper's bell and had come in to check and found her alone.

"I'll stay with her," I said.

"And I'll look for Slug," he said, going out the door. A little while later I heard his car start, and I remember wondering how David always had that car put back together when he was ready to use it.

I rubbed Harper's back, trying to quiet her, but she was still restless and seemed almost jubilant. "She came," she said. "Just this afternoon. She was here and then she left—but she did come."

"Who came, Harper?" I said, sensing that she was never going to settle down until she told someone.

"Suzanne. My daughter. I thought she never would —told Richard never to tell—but she did and I did. Told her why—how I had left her there because—and I would again. She was here and gone. In and out. But she came— I knew she would—"

After that I sat holding her hand and thinking about Slug, knowing what Harper had done to her; what I had done to her before that.

The thing about it was that part of me understood what Slug must be feeling, while the other part knew exactly why Harper did what she had to do. And I wondered when I had stopped seeing things in black and white and decided that, whenever it was, it made everything just that much more complicated.

Years ago, when I was with Monica and the rest, there were songs we sang about harmony and under-standing and love. Most of all about love. In those days we had the idea that all we had to do was want those things badly enough and we'd have them.

Well, it doesn't work that way, I thought, getting up and pushing back against the swing so that it veered crookedly off to the side before it swung forward again. And I'm sick of trying to make it work around here. Besides that, I'm hot and tired and I don't *care* where Slug is, and if she's not at Harper's by one o'clock that's Mattie-Miller's problem and not mine. I went to the edge of the porch, looking up the street, then pulled myself back, going into the house and slamming the door behind me. In the kitchen I made a glass of iced tea and carried it upstairs.

I started pulling my clothes off as I went up the steps, kicking my shoes into a corner of the hall, dropping my shirt, my belt, sure somehow that I was bound to feel more like picking them up later on. I *couldn't* feel worse. As I put the iced tea on the windowsill and started unfastening my skirt, I felt the bulge of Mattie-Miller's paperweight and took it out, turning to toss it onto the bed. Then I stopped, catching myself as the skirt slid down and lay in a blue circle around my feet. The plastic dome felt slick to the touch, and I stood rubbing it up and down the side of my face. I shook it and watched the snow storm down on a reindeer. I held it up to the light, clearing my throat, and all of a sudden, and for just a moment, I knew how Gussie must have felt when she looked at one of her treasures.

But as if I was afraid to stay too long, I broke away and hurried into the bathroom. It's too much, I thought, turning on the water and stepping into the shower. Making me think things I don't want to remember: about Gussie and Monica. About myself. And now about Slug.

As the water beat down on my back, I thought how tired I was—not just physically from being up all night with Harper, turning her, giving her medicine, a bath. More than that, I was tired of walking on eggs. Of being careful about everything I said and did.

I got out of the shower, rubbed myself dry, and put on my robe. I missed being alone, and was glad not to be alone. My house was cluttered now, with a clutter that made it more than a house. I wasn't sure how I felt about that.

I went back into my room, started for the window, and forced myself to move back, thinking about how Slug and I both just seemed to have been waiting for this year to be over and how maybe this one year was all we'd have together and that we should be doing more with it. Then I couldn't think anymore. I pulled back the spread and a terrible tiredness settled down around me.

I woke up when I heard Slug come in. The room was hot with the late-afternoon sun. My hair was wet against my head and the robe was tangled around me like a tent. She's back—she didn't leave after all, I thought, and I was out of bed and starting down the steps, feeling my relief turn to little spurts of anger.

"Where have you been?" I said, going into the kitchen.

"At Miss Tegges's," said Slug, turning to face me. "It was on the schedule," she said. "Don't we always follow the schedule around here?"

"Yes, but when I came home you weren't here; the house was empty and—" I won't say I was worried, I thought. "I was worried." I heard the words coming out of my mouth.

"Worried?" said Slug.

"Yes, worried. Is that so strange?" I said, and because I didn't want her to answer that, I hurried on. "After what happened yesterday—after what I figured out that happened yesterday. About Harper, and her daughter Suzanne, and how you must have felt about that. And when you weren't here this morning—"

"You thought I'd left?" said Slug, and I could see her turning the idea around the way I'd turned the paperweight in the sunlight.

"And I wasn't sure you'd go back, be able to go back—"

"You thought I'd left," Slug said again. "Because you left—is that why?"

"That was seventeen goddamn years ago, so give me a break." I wanted to shake her, I wanted to hug her, and Slug stepped back as if she could read my mind. I didn't know which she was more afraid of.

"Maybe it'll never work," I went on. "And at the end of this year, when Brian comes home, you'll just go to him and that'll be the end of that." I wanted to tell her that it *could* work. I was sure. Maybe. But the closed, almost blunt look on her face made me pull back. Then Slug took the conversation and turned it away from me. Her voice, when she spoke, was strangely small.

"I didn't know if I could go to see Miss Tegges today. That's why I wasn't here. Because I wasn't sure and I needed to think. To sort it out. I walked and walked, to Towson, and I don't know where else. To Gino's for breakfast and back again."

"But you went back. You did go," I said.

"Yes."

"Why?"

"Because—" and Slug stopped for a minute before going on. "Because of Miss Tegges. Because I care about her. And what happened—it was a long time ago and—"

"You could forgive her that?"

"Yes."

It was as if things exploded, and for a minute I was surprised that the words that seemed to be screaming inside my head were coming out calm and steel-edged. "If you can forgive Harper Tegges, why can't you forgive me?" I asked.

Slug

"BECAUSE you're my mother," I said. "You're my mother and you shouldn't have done it."

"But I did—" Julie said. She leaned across the table to me, so close that I could see the pores along the sides of her nose. "How long are you going to punish me for it?"

"Until . . ." I said. And then I didn't know until when.

"Until when?" Julie said. "Pigs fly? The Pope turns Jewish? Until something goddamn eats away at me the way it's doing to Harper Tegges?"

"It's got nothing to do with Miss Tegges."

"You're right. It's you and me. Just the two of us."

"And Gussie," I said.

"No. Not Gussie," she said.

And I felt excited, as if I'd been waiting for this moment all summer long. Maybe all my life.

"You could have stayed," I said.

"No."

"Why?"

"Because I was a kid with a kid."

"Me."

"How about you," Julie said. "Could you have done it any better?"

I stopped, thinking that I could have. That I would have. And suddenly not sure.

Then the phone rang.

Julie answered it, listened for a minute, and said, "I'll be right there." She put the receiver down and headed for the door, calling back over her shoulder, "Harper's had a seizure and Miss Stokes wants me to come right over."

There you go again, I thought. There you go again, I wanted to shout at the top of my lungs. Just when I need you. Just like that other time. But I knew, even as I thought it and wanted to shout it, that it wasn't like the other time. I had been a baby then and now I wasn't. Of course.

I had needed Julie, but I had had Gussie. Brian. Miss Albright. Later, Henley.

And maybe none the worse for wear.

Thoughts bounced inside my head like corn in a popper.

What she did was: right, wrong, none of the above.

Julie was gone and I ran after her, catching up just as she started up the steps to Miss Tegges's house.

"Other people did . . . would've . . . you weren't the first . . ."

"I'm not other people." Julie pulled open the door and went inside, with me just behind her.

"The seizure's over. She's all right now," Miss Stokes said in that booming whisper of hers.

Miss Tegges was lying with her eyes closed, the small brass bell in her hand.

"Afterward she was restless," Miss Stokes said, "and I gave her that."

As if she knew what we were talking about, Miss Tegges held the bell up, turning it this way and that. "There was a bell—" she said. "On Sundays, starting up and hurrying us along. Dr. Martin waiting to begin. The organ and the procession—

"Has he come?"

"Who?" said Julie, leaning close to her.

"Dr. Martin—to visit the sick. Mama used to read it out loud: 'I was sick and ye visited me.' Has he yet?"

"Would you like someone?" asked Julie. "Not Dr. Martin but someone?"

Miss Tegges plucked at an invisible thread, worrying it, pulling against the covers.

She looked at Julie and past her to Miss Stokes and me. "Yes—yes," she said. "I think it's time."

After a while she said, "They should all be here— Mama, Papa, and even Aunt Agnes, though I never much cared for her. She had whiskers." She let go of the bell and rubbed her hand over her chin.

"I don't want to be alone," she said later on.

"You're not alone," Julie said.

"It's funny, but I always *did* want to be by myself. I *had* to be. It's what I tried to tell Suzanne. But not now, not now, not now. I don't want to be alone when I die."

"You won't be alone," Julie said. "I promise you that."

Julie pulled up a chair. I saw her settle down, and I knew she was going to stay there for as long as Miss Tegges needed her. She's there for Harper Tegges, I thought, watching Julie lean forward to catch the old woman's words. But she wasn't for Gussie. For me.

I remembered how David had said to let it be. How Julie had asked how long I was going to punish her. But I still stood there, pressed against the kitchen counter.

Miss Stokes filled the water pitcher and put it on the bedside table, picking up her book and glasses and coming over to me. "I'm going," she said. "Julie'll take care of her."

Yeah, I thought. Yeah. Tell me about it. And still I stayed where I was. I watched Julie watch Miss Tegges, and thought about how Miss Tegges had left Suzanne and how I hated what she had done. And how that was only a part of her.

I looked at Julie, my mother, and wasn't at all sure

what I thought. I only knew that now, in some way, she was looking the way I had always wanted her to look.

Then I moved over to sit on the couch, still not sure of anything, and stayed there until David found me, to see if I wanted to go with him to pick up a used air conditioner for Mr. Sloane at the garage.

It was as if that day Miss Tegges had said the last thing she wanted to say, or maybe could say. I was never sure which. But from then on she lay quietly through days and nights, with hardly any difference, that stretched into weeks. As the summer skated by, I had to start thinking of starting school, Julie of going back to work, and we all wondered what we would do about Miss Tegges then. But we knew we would do something, because we hadn't come this far to give it up now.

After a while the shifts seemed to overlap, with each of us going in even when it wasn't our turn, because somehow it seemed important for us to be there. And besides that, Julie had made a promise.

David's mother took to coming over in the late afternoon, so whoever was there could go home for a shower or a little supper; and his father went to the store once to pick up a prescription, standing well back from the door when he handed it in to Julie, so he wouldn't catch anything. Even Mr. Bigelow brought flowers— zinnias, large red-and-yellow ones in a milk-glass vase

—that stayed fresh on the bookcase for the rest of Harper Tegges's life.

Miss Tegges died on a Thursday. Julie was with her, and so was I, because Julie had called for me to come.

I heard David's car and went to the door and signaled to him. He came running.

I looked at him, then back at Miss Tegges.

We waited, and after a while she was terribly still. Her eyes were closed and her right hand lay across her chest, with the other one over it protectively.

It was Julie who moved first, feeling for Miss Tegges's pulse, leaning close to her face, and going to the telephone.

The doctor came, as well as the men from the undertakers', and I stood at the back of the studio while they did what they had to do, thinking how I had done this all before, with Gussie, and not very long ago. After a while the quiet seemed to settle over the room behind me. I looked down, surprised to see that I had picked up one of Miss Tegges's paintbrushes and had dug the point over and over into the palm of my hand, leaving a trail of angry red marks.

"Well, I would say we've done our duty," Ernestus Stokes said, coming in and putting a plate of sandwiches on the kitchen counter. "I saw the car and I knew right away what had happened, so I went back inside and got this together and brought it along. At a time like this it's important to keep up one's strength." She filled the tea kettle and set it firmly on the stove.

The sun shifted in the sky and the clock on the wall inched its way along. Miss Stokes helped Julie strip the bed, and I took the sheets and pillowcases and the mattress pad across to Julie's house to the washing machine in the basement. I went back upstairs and stood at the front door, thinking back to the morning Miss Tegges fell, when Ginger had seemed to pull me along until I found her lying there.

Out on the porch I stopped at the swing Julie and I had painted, feeling for the rough places and the blisters of paint. And as I stood there all of that long summer crowded in around me.

When I got back, David and Julie had moved the hospital bed to the corner of the studio, so that when the truck came for it the men could take it out the double doors. And for a minute it seemed to me that it was all happening too fast, as if Miss Tegges were still there and they were hurrying her along. I went to the bed, holding on to the metal side rails before I moved on to the bedside table, touching her book and the bell and the glass still half filled with water.

Mattie-Miller arrived directly from work, knowing somehow, from the activity on the street, what had happened. She had a handkerchief balled in her hand, and her nose was red and twitching.

Miss Stokes took away the uneaten sandwiches and brought fresh ones and a pot of coffee.

When there was nothing left to do, we sat, suddenly awkward with one another, saying everything and nothing. David got up, pacing back and forth, stopping to look at the painting on the easel with the porch roofs and spindles, sausages in a row, and a line that was somehow like a rose.

"She called it *Street Scene*," he said. "But it was all of us, I think. And other things, too. That happens with paintings sometimes. Things you didn't plan on."

"It was all right, wasn't it?" I said, moving to stand beside him. "What we tried to do for Miss Tegges."

"We have to believe it helped, that we made it better than it could have been."

"Julie promised her that she wouldn't die alone."

"She wasn't alone," said David.

And from over on the couch came a sudden burst of sobbing. "Mattie-Miller," I said, turning to see what I could do to help.

"Come on now, David Norton, and carry these things home for me," Miss Stokes said when she had gathered up the coffeepot and sandwich plates and started for the door. David looked at me, as if he wasn't sure whether he ought to go or not.

For a minute I wanted to reach out to him and ask him to stay. Instead, I knotted my fingers behind my back and told him I'd see him later. I turned to Julie.

We finished straightening up the house, and Julie sifted through the papers in the desk to find the name of Miss Tegges's gallery so she could call them in the morning.

"We'll take the dog, for now at least," she said. "Though I don't guess whoever comes in to settle her affairs, do whatever, will care much."

Then, as if it was too soon to leave, we moved out onto the porch and sat down on the top step. One or the other of us—I don't know which and it doesn't matter anymore—reached out, and we held on to each other while the early night sounds settled down around us, and around all of Butternut Street.